Praise for *Zebra Forest*

★ "Gewirtz veers away from melodrama, deftly capturing
  nuances of family dynamics in spare prose. . . .
  Audiences will appreciate this novel's multilayered
  characters and touching message of hope and
  forgiveness." — *School Library Journal* (starred review)

"Honest and true. The tight narrative . . . is held together
with the strength of the characters." — *Booklist*

"An emotionally intense debut novel about the
complications of families. . . . The graceful narrative is
articulate and poignant, exploring through Annie's eyes
the complex grief of her family's story." — *Kirkus Reviews*

"Compelling." — *The Horn Book*

"Perfectly composed, perfectly paced — and concocted
with the perfect balance of raw emotion, brutality,
and redemption. . . . A beautiful debut."
— Jane Knight, Bear Pond Books, Montpelier, VT

"A family mystery that slowly unwinds, with doses of
suspense and intensity. . . . A skillfully crafted debut
novel from an author to watch." — *100 Scope Notes*

ZEBRA FOREST

ADINA RISHE GEWIRTZ

CANDLEWICK PRESS

Copyright © 2013 by Adina Rishe Gewirtz

First paperback edition 2014

Library of Congress Catalog Card Number 2012947251
ISBN 978-0-7636-6041-3 (hardcover)
ISBN 978-0-7636-7166-2 (paperback)

14 15 16 17 18 19 BVG 10 9 8 7 6 5 4 3 2 1

Printed in Berryville, VA, U.S.A.

This book was typeset in Minion.

Candlewick Press
99 Dover Street
Somerville, Massachusetts 02144

visit us at www.candlewick.com

For my mother, who taught me how to really *see*,
and better still, gave me the time to go looking.

And for Danny, who was the first dream that
came true, so that all the others could.

Chapter 1

Mrs. Roberts had taught sixth-grade English in my school for about eight hundred years. She was famous for cramming educational experiences into every spare minute. So on the last day of school, while the other classes had parties or played out on the field, Mrs. Roberts's English class was busy sweating the final hours away on a "surprise" end-of-year essay: "Three Wishes I'd Like to Fulfill over Summer Vacation."

Another thing about Mrs. Roberts. Not only was her end-of-school essay notorious, she never even changed the topic. So though it was supposed to be a surprise assignment for the last day of school, really every sixth grader with a normal IQ knew the question beforehand. And most had written the essay out and memorized it, because the rule in Mrs. Roberts's class was: when you were done, you could leave.

I had plenty of wishes for the summer after my sixth grade year, none of which I planned to share with Mrs. Roberts. So I wrote a fake essay for that last day, listing my wishes as:

1. See all the movies headlined at the Ace Theatre.

2. Learn to swim.

3. Visit Beth at summer camp.

None of which I wanted to do. But I did have three real wishes.

In fact, I liked Mrs. Roberts's idea so much that I'd been writing my three wishes down each summer since the year I first heard of her assignment — in the second grade.

Here were my three real wishes:

1. Get tall.

2. Have an adventure.

3. Meet my father.

Of these three wishes, none had ever been fulfilled. And, being realistic, I realized they weren't going to be. First of all, I was short and, if Gran was any indication, likely to stay that way. Combine that with my short hair and flat chest, and I looked more like an eight-year-old boy than an eleven-year-old girl and usually had to tell people my name, Annie, to make them realize the truth. But Gran says that happens when you're eleven. And since I'm not pretty, but what people call plain, I didn't think just growing my hair long would help me. Anyway, the point is, growing tall wasn't a wish that was likely to come true.

My second wish didn't hold much more hope of being fulfilled. Adventures were scarce in Sunshine, a small town of what Mrs. Roberts called "some two thousand souls," as if it were populated by ghosts. Its biggest employer was Enderfield, the state prison several miles from town; its second biggest was the local department store, Ratchett's, which was two stories high and filled with what my friend Beth liked to call Ancient Style, since everything they showed there was at least ten years out of date.

During sixth grade, the only excitement I'd had was on the few nights I got to sleep over at Beth's house and watch *The Iran Crisis: America Held Hostage* on ABC. We didn't have a TV at our house, or even a radio. The only reason we even had a telephone was because I paid our bills down at the post office, with cash Gran pulled out of various hiding places in the house. She didn't believe in dealing more than necessary with banks, which she said kept records on everybody and were nosy. So it was only by going to Beth's house that I knew those crazy Iranians had kept people hostage for 227 days by our second-to-last day of school, June 17. I'd kept count right along with Mr. Koppel, and Beth liked to marvel at the way those numbers stuck in my head. Privately, though, I thought it had more to do with only getting to watch the show three times. Things like that stay with you when you don't see them too much. Which is why my second wish wasn't exactly realistic, either. Since sitting on Beth's family-room couch and waiting for Ted Koppel to come on was the closest I had come to excitement all year, I had little hope that the summer, with Beth away at camp, would hold much adventure.

As for my third wish, I'm not even sure why I kept making it. But when you're in second grade, you don't yet know the meaning of *impossible.* And since I liked that wish best of all, I couldn't bring myself to change it, even as I grew old enough to know better.

I had no memories of my father, and not even a picture of him, since our house had no pictures. It didn't have many mirrors, either. Gran said, in one of her talkative spells, that mirrors made her uneasy. She didn't like looking into rooms she couldn't get to or at people she couldn't touch. So we had no photos, not of my father, and certainly not of my mother, who, Gran said, had run off when I was three and Rew just one.

I had one and a half memories of my mother. I say "a half" because whenever I tried to remember what my mother looked like, I saw a brown leather purse instead. That, and the sound of her keys clinking together—

that's what I remembered. And then there was the other memory, or maybe it was one Gran gave me and I made my own. That was of the night she left, when she set us down, along with our suitcases, in Gran's house. I can't see her face there, either, but I think she might have had brown hair, like mine. And I don't remember much of her voice, but I do know the words she used. "They were always his idea, anyway," she said, and left.

So I didn't miss my mother much. But my father—since I was, after all, his idea—him, I missed. And though I didn't know what he looked like, Gran said he was something like Rew, and that made a nice picture in my mind.

Rew looked like he had put his face up to the sky in a rainstorm of freckles. He was covered in them, mostly on his face, but practically every region of his body held a stray freckle or two. I envied him his freckles and his red hair, which made him stand out beside me. Stupid strangers tried to start conversations with us on the bus by asking me, "Where'd your red hair go?" As if I would love to discuss why I was boringly brown and the freckle god had been stingy with me.

So if Rew favored my father, as Gran liked to say, I could only imagine liking his face. And probably everything else about him. Rew had always fascinated me. I did most of the talking, but he did most of the thinking.

Genius and freckles must go together, because Rew got both. Even though he was only nine, most of the time he beat me at chess, a game Gran had taught us. He had a way of seeing moves ahead, so he'd trap me and checkmate me before I realized I'd been had. I won only when I could taunt him hard enough to make him mad. Rew stopped thinking when he got mad.

So I imagined my father was Rew grown big. Smart, thoughtful, freckled, red. And he was my third wish.

But that was the unlikeliest wish of all. Because even if I drank a magic elixir and sprouted a few feet, and even if angry revolutionaries suddenly stormed the streets of boring old Sunshine, making true wishes one and two, wish three was impossible. I could never meet my father. My father was dead.

Chapter 2

Rew could think better than I could, but I told the better story, probably because I was a good liar, something Gran had trained me in when I was little. We had moved to Sunshine when I was three and a half, and by the time I was five, when I could have started kindergarten with the other kids, Gran had decided to homeschool us. She didn't hold with institutions, she said, or being locked up in a big building all day. That was back when she talked more and brooded less, though she brooded often enough even then.

I must have been about six when the truant lady, or so Gran called her behind her back, came to check on us. Actually, she was a social worker named Adele Parks, who had a gentle way of talking that I liked. But I didn't get to talk to her just then. The first time she came was on one of Gran's good days, and Gran had summoned up the best of her old self, explaining to the woman, at length, her educational philosophy, which I heard her say included "lots of classics, field trips, and extensive hands-on work."

After the woman left, Gran, staring out back at the Zebra Forest, said to me, "I'm a liar, I'll admit. But I pride myself on being a real *good* liar. That's part of my educational philosophy, too, Annie B. Mark that down. Lesson one: If you're going to do something, make sure you do it with *excellence.*"

Gran's name for me, Annie B., was short for what she liked to call me: Annie Beautiful. Since I already told you I'm not one jot beautiful, that was one of Gran's lies, too. But it was one of her excellent ones. She said it so well, I sometimes believed it.

After that, Adele Parks came by most months to check in. As soon as I had learned to write, mainly by watching Gran do it and studying old *Life* magazines, I had dutifully filled out the homeschool forms she sent Gran. Of course, this only made Adele Parks a more frequent visitor, since a six-year-old filling out forms didn't inspire much confidence in the homeschooling system Gran had told her about. And so I told her lots of lies, taking my cue from Gran, but eventually she sent me, and then Rew, to the local public school.

I began in second grade, which is how I heard about

Mrs. Roberts's essay one year later than the other kids. But I found I liked school well enough, especially when I sat next to Beth Mayfield.

While I was sitting hunched in my chair that first day, Beth leaned over and told me she liked the way I wrote my name. Beth is a girl who is not afraid to ask questions, and that day, she wanted to know everything about me. I quickly found out I didn't know much about myself. Not enough to satisfy Beth, anyway.

"Where'd you move from?" she wanted to know.

"I don't know," I said, feeling foolish. "The city. I'm not sure which one."

"Well, you've got to know where you're from," Beth told me. "Ask your mother."

"I have a gran" was all I said to that.

"Ask her, then."

And so I did ask Gran. On good days, Gran would tell me plenty, but none of it answered Beth's questions. She told me about her growing up in crowded apartments where someone was always cooking, about having lots of cousins and playing marbles in the street.

Gran didn't talk like anyone else. Maybe in Chicago, where she came from, everyone sounded like her, but no one else in Sunshine could pull their words out flat, the way she did. No one else had the gravelly sound she had, even in her singing voice.

"The whole family lived in a three flat," she told Rew and me once. "That's three apartments stacked one on top of the next. And I mean uncles and aunts and grandparents and cousins—everybody. Downstairs we all worked in the family grocery. We took turns behind the counter and delivering round the neighborhood. We went where we pleased, my cousins and me. They had no playgrounds in those days. We just had the streets. The streets were ours."

"What about school?" Rew wanted to know. "Didn't you go?"

"Up till the eighth grade I did," Gran said. "Then I had to work. Everyone worked then, if they were lucky enough to have a place to."

"Weren't there truant ladies then?" I asked her.

"Oh, not then, not when I was old as that. People overestimate the amount of schooling a person needs to get by, I'd say. Look at my mother—look how she did!"

Gran's mother had run the family—all three flats of it. Gran said she was a bear of a woman—Gran called her "substantial"—and she took no lip from anyone.

Privately, Rew said "substantial" only meant fat, and that anyone who could barely read couldn't have been much of a success, but I didn't agree. In my mind's eye, Gran's mother was like Gran, only more solid. Her face was the same: eyes the color of sunny water; white, white hair; pointed nose. Wider, though. Definitely wider. Gran herself was thin, a bird of a woman, who had once been quick but who now, as the bad days grew more frequent, stayed in her chair by the window, sunk beneath her old newspapers, or upstairs, behind her closed door.

All Gran's cousins were gone now, she said, her being the youngest. There was no one left. Still, I liked to imagine her the way she must have been, a girl on the sidewalk, hair vivid red, shooting marbles and rolling pennies.

When Beth heard all this, she came the two miles from town to see Gran and our house, and she didn't mind the clutter or that Gran never threw anything out or that we mostly ate from dirty dishes or that, as time passed, I did a lot of the shopping myself, because it made Gran too tired to go into town. Beth thought our house was interesting, what with its old magazines and Gran's obsession with keeping things. And so we were friends.

That was enough for me. And Gran said I ought to be grateful and not wish the other kids would come by, or want to, even.

"I don't like people snooping around," she said. "We're enough for each other, aren't we?"

I always told her yes, of course we were. And on her good days, it was even true. But by the end of sixth grade, I'd counted more bad days than good, more days when Gran didn't wake until noon, and then only got up to sit in the kitchen, staring through the windows at the Zebra, grinding the tip of her slipper into the linoleum until it left little bits of gray rubber scattered like eraser dust on the floor. So I looked forward to summer less than I had. But still, there was good in it. There was Rew, and there was the Zebra, where the two of us would go each day, and tell stories, and climb trees, and listen to uncluttered quiet that had no warning in it.

So as that summer began, while America counted hostage days and Beth learned to swim, I thought up good lies to tell and climbed trees and lay a lot in the shade. I didn't think any of my wishes would come true, not even the one about getting taller.

Chapter 3

We called it the Zebra Forest because it looked like a zebra. Its trees were a mix of white birch and chocolate oak, and if you stood a little ways from it, like at our house looking across the back field that was our yard, you saw stripes, black and white, that went up into green.

Gran never went out there except near dusk, when the shadows gathered. She usually didn't go out in full sunlight, and told me once she didn't like the lines the trees made. Gran was always saying stuff like that. Perfectly beautiful things—like a clean blue sky over the Zebra—made tears come to her eyes, and if I tried to get her to come outside with me, she'd duck her head and hurry upstairs to bed. But then it would be storming, lightning sizzling the tops of the trees, and she'd run

round the house, cheerful, making us hot cocoa and frying up pancakes and warming us with old quilts.

We had few rules in our house, but keeping out of the
Zebra Forest in a storm was one of them. In fact, I'd be
hard pressed to list any other rules at all, maybe because
aside from that, we didn't think to do much that Gran
would have minded. She never cared if we went to
school, and lots of times I didn't. If I missed half a week,
Adele Parks would come around, asking if I wasn't feeling well. And of course I'd hack and cough then, double
over in pain and tell her I'd had a fever of 106 just that
morning but that it seemed to be lifting and so I'd be
back in a few days. And then I'd go back again, but only
because I wanted to. Once I missed two whole weeks,
because I happened to know Adele Parks had gone off
to visit her sick mother out of town. Before she left, she
made me promise I'd go to school while she was gone,
but she probably knew that didn't mean much. I only did
go back because Beth said she wouldn't visit after school
if I didn't come at least once in a while.

Adele Parks liked to talk to me about responsibility,
a topic that bored me. I figured as long as Rew and I each
knew enough to pass into the next grade, we were fine.

"You need to buckle down, Annie," she'd say. "You
could really do something with that mind of yours."

What Adele Parks didn't seem to realize was that I used my mind plenty. I used it to tell Rew stories.

Every day after school, once we'd gone out and settled ourselves in the Zebra, he'd look at me with expectation, and I'd have to think. That's how Rew was — it took thinking to keep him happy.

Since he'd been little, Rew loved two things: jokes and pirate stories. He'd gotten attached to jokes when he found an old joke book among Gran's stacks. And when he'd finished that, he thought up his own.

They were always awful.

"What did the limestone say to the geologist?" he'd ask me.

"That's not a joke," I'd say. "It's a riddle."

"You just don't know. Come on, what did it say?"

"I don't know. Tell me."

Rew would grin. "Don't take me for granite!"

He'd laugh at himself then, since I wasn't about to. "Get it? Granite?"

I would usually groan and fall back against the nearest tree. "How can someone so smart love such stupid jokes?" I'd ask him.

And he'd laugh again. "Actually, that was a riddle. Want to hear a joke now?"

"No!"

"Fine, tell me a story, then."

He'd started loving pirate stories in kindergarten, when he found *Treasure Island* in Gran's bedroom. Or rather half of *Treasure Island*. The first seven chapters were gone from it, ripped out neat at the binding, and so we began at chapter 8, "At the Sign of the Spy-glass." Rew was too little to read such a hard book himself, so I read it to him, and we both loved to hear about Jim Hawkins, treasure maps, and Long John Silver. After a while, I offered to get the book out of the public library so we could see how it all started, but Rew preferred to imagine how Jim Hawkins had got himself mixed up with pirates. So we started to tell ourselves new beginnings, out in the Zebra.

Each of us had our favorite people in the story, and we liked to imagine what they'd done before they all boarded the *Hispaniola*. Even when I grew interested in some of the other books I found in Gran's piles, about spunky girls who tamed wild horses or geniuses who used math to predict the future, Rew couldn't get enough of pirates, and he even wanted to hear stories about the terrible blue-faced Captain Flint, who'd killed his men and hidden the treasure.

I couldn't say I loved the pirates, exactly, but I loved the story, and so I'd take turns making things up and going back to the book, where I never got tired of seeing Jim Hawkins get home with that treasure in the end.

As for Rew, he knew who the good guys were, and he liked Jim Hawkins all right, but he was most of all stuck on Long John Silver. I'd tried to explain to him, when we first read it, how bad old Long John was, but Rew wouldn't have any of it. He agreed, of course, that Long John was a bad man. But that old sea cook was just so *smart*, Rew kept coming back to him.

"You can't trust him, though," I said.

Rew liked him just the same.

And of course, there were other things that drew us to *Treasure Island*. For one thing, we could never get enough of the way they swore. "Shiver me timbers" and "By the powers!" We loved that stuff. When those pirates got mad — which was a lot — they spouted "oaths," as Jim Hawkins called them. Rew loved that word, too, because he thought it sounded like "oaks"— the kind out in the Zebra. But I looked it up in the dictionary and told him it meant "promises," which stumped us.

"What's he promising to do? What kind of promise is 'Shiver me timbers' or 'By the powers'?" he asked me.

I had no idea, but that didn't stop either of us from spouting oaths ourselves.

Rew loved pirates so much, he started seeing them everyplace.

"Do you think Gran was a pirate once?" he asked me one day, when he had just turned seven.

"Course not!" I said, surprised. "Gran? Why would you think so?"

"She keeps her treasure hidden. Just like Captain Flint on Treasure Island."

I laughed. "She didn't get it from being a pirate," I told him. "Grandpa gave it to her, before he died."

On one of her most talkative days, Gran had told me that. In the city that had no name, my grandfather had died, just before we came to Sunshine.

"He was a good man," Gran had said that time. "But his heart couldn't take it."

"Take what?" I'd asked her.

"Living."

Gran's answers were like that sometimes, and when they were, the story was over. But I knew my grandpa had taken care of Gran, leaving her money to live on if something happened to him, because she'd told me so, told me he was a careful man who always took care. And so she'd gathered up Rew and me, and the money he'd left her, and come to Sunshine, far away from the place where living was too much for Grandpa Snow.

Rew didn't want to hear about a grandpa with a hurt

heart, though. And so one day that year I agreed that our grandpa *had* been a pirate and that Gran got her treasure from a treasure box he'd left, which was still buried out on the edge of the Zebra.

"Is that why she lets everyone call her Morgan?" he asked me, thinking it over. "Like Adele Parks and them?"

When we had first registered for school, Gran had put us down under the name Morgan, which had been her name before she married Grandpa Snow, when she lived in Chicago. "My mother would have liked to be remembered that way" was all she said about it. And that was Gran. But at home, she never let us forget that we were Snows, and neither of us would have had it any other way. Snow had been our father's name, after all.

"That's right," I told Rew. "See, pirates never use their real names. You think Long John Silver's mother *named* him that? Course not. So Grandpa Snow's pirate name was Morgan, and he stamped that name right on his big treasure box, with the special seal pirates use. If Gran didn't use that name Morgan, that box wouldn't *budge* open. And so she keeps her pirate name, and that's how she gets at the treasure."

Rew grinned. "The old pirate Morgan. That's a great name. Where'd he sail? In the Atlantic?"

"He sailed down to the islands," I told him. "To the Bermuda Triangle, where ships get lost at sea."

"And is that what happened to him? Did his ship get lost?"

I nodded. "Absolutely," I said. "It's a mystery right to this day. His ship was swallowed up, and no one ever saw it again."

Chapter 4

The stories about Grandpa Snow's days as a pirate lasted us weeks, the year Rew turned seven. But the stories I made up about the great pirate Morgan were nothing compared to the ones I told about his son, Andrew. Our father.

Because it turned out that once I started, I couldn't stop telling Rew things about people that were only sort of real. And of all the people we wanted to hear about, both of us, Andrew Snow was top on the list.

By the time I was halfway through sixth grade, I had taken my father through at least three careers, not even counting the one about him being the son of a pirate. Andrew Snow had been a pilot, breaking the sound barrier somewhere near Hawaii. (I liked that location especially after I'd seen a picture of it in one of the ancient encyclopedias Gran kept under a side table in the front room.) He'd been a miner, too, surviving a cave-in deep in the hills of Kentucky by digging himself out with his hands. One year he'd been a hurdler in the Olympics, missing the gold medal only because he hit the final hurdle as he leaped it, losing a fraction of a second. Things like that count in the Olympics.

Most recently he was a secret agent, working to free those hostages in Iran. Rew loved to imagine the Middle Eastern desert, sandstorms and mullahs and veiled ladies, and our father somewhere among them, bartering for hostages in a dusty marketplace or smoking a hookah with a sheik. I knew, of course, that the hostage takers wore regular clothes and carried machine guns. I'd seen that at Beth's house, on ABC. But I also knew Rew wouldn't believe in any bad guys who wore slacks and V-neck sweaters. So the way I told it, Secret Agent Snow had sword fights with wild-bearded men in long robes. I threw in the occasional sand viper, too, because I'd read about them in an old *National Geographic* I'd found wedged behind the tank in the bathroom.

I began our summer story on the fifth day of vacation, after watching Beth's bus leave for camp. We'd already put school away, which in our house meant throwing our books into a pile. In my bedroom, my second-grade notebooks formed the base of a tower as high as my bed, right beside some of Gran's old newspapers, a lot of which had migrated in from the hall. I did often think of clearing out that space, imagining my room clean and airy like Beth's, instead of dark and smelling of old paper. But something usually distracted me before I actually did anything about it.

Besides, the Zebra was clear, and that's where we told our stories, anyway.

"It's day two hundred thirty-three," I began, taking my cue from ABC. "Agent Andrew Snow is riding by camel to a distant village, just on the edge of the desert."

Rew took great pride in my father's full name, since of course it was his name, too, Rew being short for Andrew. Because of that, and because we'd never known our father in person, we never spoke of him as Dad or Pop or any of those names kids call their fathers. Besides, it didn't seem to me someone called Dad would enter the space program or ride bareback across the Sierra Nevada.

"When he arrives, he looks out over all that sand, and he squints, like this."

I showed him Andrew Snow's trademark squint, left eye closed, right eye open.

"Like a pirate!" Rew said.

"Yeah, like a pirate," I told him. I explained that Andrew Snow had a bit of a weakness in his left eye, having hurt it during that cave-in in Kentucky.

Rew thought about that. "Gran does it, too," he said. "I've seen her, when she's looking close at something."

"Well, maybe I'm wrong. Maybe *she* was the pirate, and not old Morgan," I said. "Do you want me to go on, or not?"

Rew quieted down.

I continued. "Andrew Snow squinted out at the desert, shielding his eyes from the sand whipping up at him. Like this." Again, I closed my left eye and shaded my right. "Can't get sand in that good eye," I said. "And he laughed — one loud bark of a laugh, like this." I laughed, loud, and the sound of it echoed off the nearest trees.

"Why did he laugh?" Rew wanted to know.

"Because he knew something those Iranians didn't know," I said. "He knew there was a secret path into the embassy, and that's what he could see, looking out in the desert."

"A secret path through the desert?" Rew asked. "Isn't it all just sandy and flat, filled with sand vipers and scorpions?"

"Well, yeah, but not all of it," I said. "There was an oasis out there, and Andrew Snow knew it. One thing about Andrew Snow, he always comes prepared. He makes plans."

"Except in Kentucky," Rew reminded me.

"You can't plan a cave-in," I said. Sometimes it was hard to tell Rew stories; he was so particular. "But he got out, didn't he?"

Rew nodded. "He did. That's true."

I sighed. "Any more questions, or should I keep going?"

This was our routine. I'd begin a story, and Rew would take apart every piece of it, check it to make sure it made sense, drive me crazy, then let me go on.

"Keep going," he said. "Of course keep going."

"Okay. So Andrew Snow had looked into everything, even before he went," I told him. "That old desert was just riddled with tunnels and underground caves — like the kind in *Ali Baba* and *Aladdin*. And there were ancient maps of some of them, which Andrew Snow knew how to get. So he knew there was one that went right to the embassy, all the way back in the capital. And that's how he was going to get at those hostages."

As I described Andrew Snow's sunburned face and his amazing mastery of Farsi — his skill in languages having been passed down to him by his father, the old pirate Morgan, who had learned ancient scripts so he could read treasure maps — I wondered whether my father had known any languages, or what kind of job he'd really done. Because actually I knew next to nothing about Andrew Snow, hurdler, test pilot, secret agent. I didn't because I lied earlier, when I said I couldn't remember any other rules in our house besides not going into the Zebra during a storm. There was one, and though we never spoke of it, we knew it better than any other.

That was that we didn't talk about our father, not in the house. Gran had told me one story about him, a long time ago, when I was too young to know what not to ask. The telling of it had sent her to her room for days, nearly a week, during which time the milk went sour and Rew and I were reduced to eating nothing but dry cereal and raw macaroni, since we didn't yet know how to use the stove.

The story was of the night my father died. On that night, Andrew Snow had met an angry man, who picked a fight, then beat him. My father died and the other man was sent away, and that was all. The end. The story of my father was a short one.

And so I knew these things about Andrew Snow. I knew he had had two good ideas: Rew and me. And I knew that someone angry had killed him.

Chapter 5

Whenever Gran had a good spell, life got a lot more interesting. That summer, Gran had a long stretch of good days—nearly two weeks—in which she stocked up on groceries, set the table with good china, and even taught us how to play gin rummy, with eleven cards, the hard way.

"The seven-card game is for people who can't manage their cards, Annie B.," she told me. "You can do eleven just fine."

Up until that point, Gran's favorite card game had been blackjack, which she could play for a full day, until Rew and I were practically wild with boredom. But gin rummy had a little more give to it, what with the different ways you could match the cards. What I liked especially about it was that right from the start, I kept winning.

Rew hated it. "It's a stupid game," he whispered to me when Gran, during one particularly long gin-rummy binge, excused herself to go to the bathroom. "It's nothing but luck."

"Not true," I said. "You've got to think about which cards to throw out and which to keep. You've got to take your chances on that."

He snorted. I knew right away why Rew was no good at gin rummy. He held on to his cards too long. If he made up his mind to collect jacks, he wouldn't give over, even when I had held one or two in my hand so long, we'd have to turn the pile over and start again. He kept hoping I'd give them to him.

"Chances, right," he said. "Like I said, it's just luck. At least in chess, if you think hard enough, you win."

Since I couldn't think hard enough to beat him at chess, I didn't contradict him. But I still took some satisfaction in my success at cards. And besides, Rew didn't stay mad too long. He couldn't, what with Gran so cheerful.

One morning, she sat on the floor, sifting through her magazines, and pulled out one of our mutual favorites, *Life*, 1949, the October 31st issue. Pretty Princess Margaret posed on the front of that one, looking sadly off into the distance.

Gran studied her face, though we'd both seen the

picture at least a million times. "Sad life," she said. "Unhappy lady."

I'd heard the story of Princess Margaret any number of times, but it was one of Gran's favorites, and when she was in a good mood, I always liked the sound of her voice. So I asked, "How come?"

"She was a royal lady, and she fell in love with a captain in the Royal Air Force. Very handsome. They wanted to get married, but they couldn't."

"Why not?" I prompted.

"He was a divorced man, and in those days, when you might be queen, you couldn't marry somebody like that."

I'd thought a lot about Princess Margaret since the first time Gran showed me her picture. So I said, "If it were me, I'd have married him anyway."

Gran sighed. "Well," she said, "Princess Margaret felt responsible to her people, being in line for the throne, you know. She gave him up for duty. But then, of course, some say her sister made her do it."

"She sounds like a bad lady," I said to Gran.

"Maybe," she said. "Some people are too much about responsibility. But then, some people are too little."

I thought she must mean me, so I said, "Well, did Margaret ever get to be queen, after all that?"

Gran shrugged and tucked the magazine back into

the pile, where it stayed, somewhere between the edition on Joe DiMaggio and the one on Judy Garland. "No," she said. "I don't think she ever did."

That night we had a dinner party with the good china, pretending we were royal and dining in the palace. Even though Gran had taken to washing the dishes that week, this time, she laughed and said the footmen would clear.

Chapter 6

Even on her best days, Gran went to bed when it turned dark. She didn't like how the windows reflected our faces back, as if we were outside, looking in. So that night, after our happy dinner, when Gran went upstairs, I gave in to Rew and sat on the floor with the chessboard, getting beaten again and again.

Finally I gave up. We left the board on the floor, and Rew sat over it, arranging and rearranging the pieces, moving his queen back and forth. I settled myself on the couch, lying on my stomach, chin on my hands, and fell asleep watching him.

I woke to a noise. The lights were still on, and Rew was asleep on the floor, head between a couple of stray pawns.

Someone was rattling the back door, in the kitchen. We never locked it, but it stuck, and if you rattled it once or twice, it opened. I got up, stepping on Rew in the process, and made my way to the kitchen just as the back door opened, and a man stepped in.

I blinked, trying to make sense of him. Behind him, I could see the white lines of the Zebra Forest shimmering in the moonlight. My heart started to shake inside my chest. I heard Rew come from the front room.

The man stood very still, looking at us, trying to focus his eyes in the sudden light. The first things I noticed about him were his red hair and the mud on his face. In fact, he was caked in mud, as if he'd fallen in it. He wore a torn beige shirt, thick slacks, and heavy shoes.

Before I could think what to do, the man turned, locked the kitchen door, and pocketed the key we always kept in the back of the knob.

"Just stay quiet and I won't hurt anybody," he said. "I'll stay only as long as I need. Just stay quiet and you'll be fine."

I couldn't think what he meant. But Rew, always quick, understood immediately. Behind me, I heard him dash into the front room and grab the phone.

The man was quicker. He shoved past me, rushed at Rew, and knocked the phone from his hands. It fell with a clang, taking the end table with it. Rew scrambled after it, but the man threw him aside, yanked at the phone cord, and ripped it sharply from the wall. Then he threw the phone out of reach, and the house echoed with the sound of its bell as it hit the wall.

Rew turned and ran for the front door. He fumbled with the lock, his hands shaking. I darted forward to help him, but the man grabbed at me as I passed, catching me by the hair. He jerked me back so hard, I lost my footing and fell against him, my head slamming against his ribs. Then his heavy arm came round my throat, and with his free hand he grabbed my arms and held me tight to his chest as I struggled to pull away. I kicked back as hard as I could, but his arm squeezed my throat and I held still, gagging.

"Stop!" he yelled at Rew, who had nearly gotten the front door open. "Go anywhere or call anyone and I'll hurt her! You see? I will!"

And he crushed me with that arm, making me choke and struggle again.

Rew froze. He took his hand from the door.

"That's it," the man said. And I could feel, against my back, the furious beating of his heart. "I don't want to hurt anybody, like I said. Don't make me."

I tried to say something, but the arm across my neck tightened until I could do nothing but rasp. I could almost see Rew's chess mind working behind his eyes. Something had dawned on him. "You're from the prison," he said quietly. "Back there."

I could feel the man nod. "And they're looking for me, but they won't look here. There was a riot earlier tonight, and a lot of guys broke out. Most of them went up the highway. That's where they'll go. No one else went for the woods. So if you just stay patient, I'll wait it out, and I'll go in a while. It won't be long. Stay quiet, and you'll be fine, and I'll go away."

If he hadn't had his arm round my throat, I'd have thought the man was pleading with Rew, not threatening him.

Rew had no choice. "All right," he said, taking a step from the door. "Don't hurt her."

We stood there like that for a long time, until I could feel the man's heart slow, against my back. Gradually, he loosened his grip on my throat. But he didn't let go. I took a breath, inhaling the sour smell of his sweat and the soft odor of mud that reminded me of the Zebra Forest.

Rew still stood looking at him, unsure what to do next. Finally, he asked, "Will you go in the morning?"

I knew he was thinking of Gran. Neither of us wanted to think what she would do if she came down in the morning and found an escaped prisoner holding us hostage.

"Not in the morning," the man said, and now I wondered why he still held me, when he would let go. "But as soon as it's safe. I'm leaving the country. I can't travel for at least a week, though. Maybe more."

If Rew could have gotten any paler, he did just then. His freckles stood out against his suddenly white skin. There was no way to keep this terrible stranger secret from Gran for a week. Not in one of her good spells.

But as it turned out, we couldn't even keep him secret for an hour, because while we were all standing there, looking at each other, Gran came halfway down the stairs. And now she stood there in her nightgown, staring at the stranger behind my head. And she said the last thing either Rew or I would have ever expected.

"Andrew Snow," she said. "Let go of my Annie B."

Chapter 7

I'd known Gran to go silent. I'd known her to close her door and not come out for days, not even to eat. But I'd never known her to see things that weren't there. Now I thought, *This strange man has taken Gran's mind. It's gone.*

Rew clearly thought the same thing. In a voice so gentle and steady you wouldn't think a mud-splattered convict had just stormed our house and taken us prisoner, he said, "No, Gran, this isn't Andrew Snow. This is a man who came from the prison. On the other side of the Zebra."

He said it as if the man whose arm still pressed against my throat had come for a friendly visit. A cup of tea.

But Gran was coming down the stairs. She acted like she hadn't heard him. She came close to me, to the man, and peered up at him.

"Andrew," she said. "Let her go. This is Annie."

I was about to try and tell the man that my grandmother wasn't in her right mind just then. That he ought to go and find some other house to hide out in, because he was only making her worse, and here she'd been having a good spell. But before I could say any of that, before I could say even one word, the man's arm dropped from my throat. He let me go.

I stumbled away from him, away from Gran, too, who still stood close to him, looking up into his face. Rew came to help me, and when I was steadier, we turned to look at them. Gran was still staring intently at the man, searching his face for something, but he wasn't looking back at her. He was looking, instead, at me. At me and Rew.

"I didn't know," he said, and his voice seemed to tremble. "I didn't know you were here."

A buzzing started in my ears just then. Gran once quoted some writer who said, "The blood will out." I'd never really understood what she meant. But now I think it must mean that your blood knows things before your head does. Because even as I struggled to make sense of Gran's words, and the man's, the blood came rushing into my head, making me dizzy.

Rew, of course, understood right away. And his voice sounded like it came from under water when he said, "*You?* You're Andrew Snow?"

And through my swimming eyes, I saw the man in the muddy prison uniform nod.

He was Andrew Snow. Andrew Snow. Our father.

And I realized suddenly, a minute after my blood did, that our father hadn't been killed by an angry man, like Gran had said.

He was the angry man.

Chapter 8

Liar!" Rew screamed. "You're a liar!"

For a minute, I couldn't figure out who he was screaming at, but the man knew.

"No," he said. "It's true."

"You're not Andrew Snow!" Rew yelled again. "Our father's dead. Gran said it! Somebody killed him. He's dead."

The man looked at Gran, then back at Rew. "Last time I saw you, you were just a baby," he said wonderingly.

Rew looked like he had gone mad. His eyes bulged and his face flushed, and he shook his head fast, again and again.

"Gran! Tell him! Tell him what happened to our father!"

Gran had begun to shiver. She shook so hard, she had to sit down, and the man helped her to the couch. As for me, I felt like I'd stepped out of my own body. The rushing in my head was so loud, I could only just hear what people said, and Rew's screaming sounded like it was a million miles away. I looked at the man, and at Gran, and Rew, but they seemed almost as if they stood behind thick glass, acting out a play I could just barely hear.

"Andrew, Andrew," Gran was saying, again and again. "You're back."

"He's not!" Rew shouted. "He's not! Don't say that! He's a bad man! This man ran away from the prison!"

At that Gran shook harder. "You didn't, you didn't," she said. "Did you, Andrew? Did you?" '

The man stood there, face whiter and whiter, hands clenching and unclenching, looking down at Gran.

"I did," he said. "There was a riot. I — I just ran."

Gran put her head in her hands. "No," she said. "No, you couldn't have."

Rew looked with horror at Gran, rocking there on the couch. "Make him get out!" he screamed at her. "He's a liar! Make him get out!"

Gran put her hands over her ears and rocked harder.

The rushing sound began to die in my head as I watched her. I could hear Rew now, gulping air as if he'd just been running, and the man, Andrew Snow, breathing heavily too, watching Gran, watching us.

"Get out!" Rew screamed at him. "Both of you! Both of you! Liars! Liars!"

Gran lifted her head at that. She looked at him, and her lips trembled.

I yanked at Rew's arm.

"Stop it!" I whispered. "Stop it! Be quiet!"

But Rew wouldn't be quiet. He rushed at the man and shoved him hard. Though Rew was less than half his size, the man hadn't been expecting it, and he staggered back.

"Get out!" Rew screamed at him. "Get out!"

Gran began to wail. I had never heard her cry before, and after all the things I had seen that night, this sound, more than anything, made me afraid.

Her wail was jagged and high-pitched, and she rocked back and forth, crying.

It made Rew pause for a moment, and the man, his face slick now with sweat, rushed at Rew and jerked him off his feet.

"Stop it," he said, gripping Rew so tight his knuckles whitened. His voice had gone hard again. "Stop it. I'm not going. I'm here now, and I'm going to stay here. Stop it, or I'll make you stop." With each word, he seemed to squeeze Rew tighter, and I ran over and tried to pry his fingers loose, but he just shook me off.

He'd pulled Rew in close to his face, but at the last word, he shoved him away, sending Rew careening past the overturned end table. I caught my brother by the shoulders just before he fell and helped him right himself.

He was okay, but Gran wasn't. Her crying had turned into jagged sobbing, as if she couldn't get enough air in. I wanted to cover my ears like she did, and run from it. But instead, when I let go of Rew, I turned and took her arm.

"Gran," I said. "Gran, come upstairs. It's okay. No one's going to hurt us. We're okay."

Gran hunched over so far, her head touched her knees.

"Gran," I said again, tugging at her arm. "Come on, now."

Her crying grew softer, and after a little bit, she let me pull her from the couch and lead her upstairs. I laid her down in her bed, covered her with her quilts, and left her there, whimpering, curled like a baby and clutching her own hands tight, one to the other.

When I came downstairs, Andrew Snow and Rew still stood in the front room, glaring at each other. With a sudden shock, I realized that one thing Gran had said was true. Andrew Snow did look something like Rew, with his red hair and his pale face.

I looked back upstairs, at the closed door of Gran's room. And I knew that Gran had told me the truth all along. She had always said she was a good liar. Only until that night, I'd never known just how good a lie she could tell. Just how good a liar she was.

Chapter 9

The three of us spent the night in the living room. I don't know when I fell asleep, but I woke to the sound of a chair toppling. In the night, Andrew Snow had pushed it up against the door. Now he'd just jumped up from it. He stood beside the front window, peering out.

I could hear an engine outside and got to my feet to look past him, out the window. Down the road, a police car was just turning at the end of the long, muddy drive that led up to our house. Andrew Snow jerked back at the sight of it, then looked wildly at me and Rew. Rew, who had fallen asleep beside me on the couch, was just lifting his head.

"You have a cellar?" Andrew Snow demanded. "A basement?"

I couldn't help looking backward toward the kitchen, where the door to our rarely used basement was tucked between the table and the stove. That was all the answer Andrew Snow needed. He ran at us then, grabbing both me and Rew and dragging us toward the kitchen. Rew didn't even have a second to get his bearings before Andrew Snow gave him a little shake.

"Open it!" he said. "Now."

Rew wouldn't. He tried to pull away, but, watching Andrew Snow's face, I knew it would be better just to listen. So I did it. I didn't want him pushing Rew.

We hated going down to the cellar. It smelled of wet, and Rew thought there were rats down there. I was more familiar with it, though, since our washing machine was down there and I used it every week. I'd never seen a rat, but I did hate the bare pipes and the stinky old sofa Gran kept there, plus all the old clothes and other garbage that smelled of mothballs and damp.

Still, I opened the door — and got a faceful of stale air before Andrew Snow hustled us down into the dark. In the cellar, the only light from outside filtered through a rusted old vent in the wall just over the couch.

Andrew Snow saw it and pushed us that way. He looked around the room, and I wondered if he was searching for something to tie us with. But instead he whipped us around and pulled us down onto the smelly cushions with him, clamping a firm hand over both our mouths.

Above us, through the vent, I could hear the police car pull up and the engine cut off. Doors slammed.

"Just keep quiet, and we'll all be fine," Andrew Snow whispered. "No one's going to bother us down here."

I could feel the stubble of his face against the side of my head. He still smelled of mud and sweat. I tried to pull away, but it was no use. Rew squirmed and tried to twist out of Andrew Snow's grip, but he had us with those arms of his. I took a try at biting the hand over my mouth, but Andrew Snow didn't even flinch. So I kicked him, and then Rew did, too.

He grunted, and I felt satisfied for a minute, then scared, thinking he might kick back. Instead, he lifted his legs and wrapped them tight over ours, pressing our feet into the base of the couch. No matter how we wriggled and tried to pull at his arms, he didn't budge.

Upstairs, the policemen were ringing the doorbell.

Gran won't answer, I thought, *and they'll break down the door.*

Break it down! I thought.

"You think no one's home?" one of them said. Their voices came through the vent clearly.

"This early?" another voice said. "No, ring it again. And knock."

The doorbell echoed through the house, followed by a loud banging.

Break it, I pleaded silently.

"We'd better call it in," the first one said. "See if we ought to get in here."

"Try it again," the other one answered. "It's early yet."

Behind me, I could hear Andrew Snow's harsh breathing.

What would he do when they came for him? Would he try to run? Would they shoot him?

I wanted to turn my head and look at Rew, see if he was thinking the same thing. Did he want them to shoot Andrew Snow? Did I?

But I couldn't turn my head. Andrew Snow held it too tight. His heart was beating twice as fast as it had the night before. Were they going to break the door down?

Then we heard someone overhead. Gran. I could tell by the shuffling sound of her footsteps that she was wearing her slippers. And then she was at the door.

"Yes?" we heard her say.

The first policeman must have been consulting his notes, because it took a second for him to answer. "Miz Morgan?" he said. "Could you open up? We'd like to talk to you a minute."

We heard the door open. "Certainly, come on in," Gran said. I tried to listen for the strain in her voice but realized with a start that she had her liar's voice on.

The same steady voice she used with Adele Parks on the good days.

Tell them, I pleaded silently. *Tell them to take him and just put him back. No shooting.*

But Gran didn't say that. Instead, she said, "Would either of you like a drink or something?"

"No, ma'am," the first policeman said, and now that they were inside, I had to strain to hear them. "We're just checking on all the houses in the area. I don't know if you heard, but there was a prison break last night over at Enderfield."

Gran didn't miss a beat. "Really? No, I don't get the news much. No TV."

"Yes, well, we're checking on all the neighbors, just to be sure they're all right."

I heard the creak of the sofa overhead. Someone must have sat down. Maybe Gran.

"Should I be worried?" she asked.

"No, ma'am, we don't think so." It was the second policeman who answered. "In most of these cases, the ones who run want to get as far away as quick as they can. Most of them went up toward the bigger cities, and we've got a fugitive alert for them up there."

"Well," Gran said, "that's good to hear."

"Do you mind if we take a look around, ma'am? Just to go over things?"

Gran didn't answer right away, and I heard the sofa creak again.

If I could have held my breath, I would have, but since Andrew Snow's sweating hand was already nearly smothering me, I couldn't afford to. Instead, I closed my eyes, to hear better. I wondered if Gran would give the least hint that they ought to look — that things weren't okay.

But she answered, "Oh, certainly. Please forgive the mess."

"Oh, no, Miz Morgan, we only meant outside. We'll go around back and take a look."

"Oh, certainly," she said again. "If you want to go through the house, the kitchen door's that way."

They'd pass the cellar door if they went that way. Had Andrew Snow closed it? Rew must have been thinking the same thing, because he started trying to kick again. But the first policeman said, "That's all right — we'll go around the house. Thanks for your time, Miz Morgan. And just in case, make sure you keep your doors locked for the next few days. I tell you there's nothing to worry about, but if you see anything to make you the least bit concerned, you give us a call at this number."

I thought for a minute how strange it was that the first time anyone ever told us to worry about locking our doors was when Andrew Snow had already gotten in and locked us in with him.

We heard footsteps again overhead, and the front door close. Outside, the policemen's voices grew clearer, near the vent.

"Well," the second one said, "three more houses, and then it's a clean sweep. Every one of them up the highway. What a mess."

"Be glad you don't work at the prison," the other one said as they moved off.

I felt sick. Between the taste of Andrew Snow's sweaty hand against my mouth, the stink of the old couch, and the mothbally basement, I thought I might retch. But it must have been Andrew Snow's lucky day, because I didn't. Instead, I felt myself going greener and greener as the minutes ticked by. Rew kept squirming every once in a while, but I was too nauseous even to try moving. Finally, we heard the policemen again. They'd made their way back to their car. We listened as the doors creaked open and slammed shut, the engine revved to life, and they drove off, down our muddy front lane.

The police car had been out of earshot for five full minutes before Andrew Snow let us go. All that time, sick and smothered by his hand, I kept thinking, *Where is Gran?* But she didn't come looking. She didn't even call out to us.

Chapter 10

Andrew Snow marched us upstairs and went straight to rebolt the front door. Then he put his chair against it again. Rew and I stood blinking in the light of the kitchen. Neither of us said a word. My head still felt funny, and my stomach worse. I sat down in one of the kitchen chairs and pressed my cold hands against my forehead, trying to right myself.

Rew leaned over me, tugging a little at my arm.

"You okay? Did he choke you too much?"

I tried to shake my head, but it made my stomach lurch. So I said, "No, it's just the stink of that old basement. I hate that couch." I looked at him from the corners of my eyes and tried to smile, but I could see his relief quickly turning to fury again. He looked up, past me, into the living room.

"She cares more about him than she does us," he said.

With an effort, I lifted my head and followed his gaze. Gran was sitting there, still, on the couch. But she hadn't spoken to Andrew Snow. She looked frozen, staring out the window. As for Andrew Snow, he seemed to find his hands extremely interesting, because he didn't raise his head once.

My stomach was beginning to settle, and I took a deep breath. "Maybe she was afraid they'd shoot him or something," I said quietly.

But I could see Rew working himself up. His face had gone blotchy. Ever since he was little, Rew's face would go red and white and his freckles would stand out when he got mad. He'd been white-faced when we'd come from downstairs. Now the red was coming out.

"She's worried, Rew," I told him, getting more worried myself by the minute. "That's all. That's why she sent them away. She won't let him do anything to us."

But Rew was so mad, tears started in his eyes. And Rew was tough. Once, in third grade, he'd been bullied so badly in school, I found him curled up in the back of the bus, nursing a big scrape he'd gotten down one arm when some bigger kid pushed him off the jungle gym. And he hadn't even cried then. Now the tears only made him angrier.

"I *hate* her," he said. He raised his voice a little with

every word, and the red from his face crept right down his neck. "I hate both of them. They *both* should go to jail. I wish the both of them were *dead*."

The first time I'd ever done our shopping, I was nine, Rew's age. Gran had given me a list and money, and told me it would be okay, she just couldn't manage to go into town that day. But I was nervous, thinking of the big grocery store I'd been in with her, the one on the end of town, and so I took Rew with me. When we got there, the place was so big and bright, Rew got overexcited. While I read the list, trying to figure out the aisles, Rew followed some woman who had a little dog in her cart, and when I turned around for him, he was gone.

I called him, but he didn't come. And I got a feeling then, a sudden, terrified feeling, like nothing would ever be okay again. Nothing would ever be good. It settled right inside my throat and squeezed so tight, I could barely speak up enough for the cashier to hear me when I asked for help finding my brother. She paged him over the intercom, and we found him not far away, standing by the fresh-flower display. We got home all right; we even got our groceries. But I never forgot that feeling, so sudden and awful.

That was the feeling that hit me in the kitchen.

Because I looked up when Rew said that, about wishing Gran were dead. And I saw Gran. She was turned around on the couch, staring straight at us, her eyes big.

Rew saw her, too, but it didn't stop him. He walked right into the living room, up to one of the side tables beside the couch, where a stack of her favorite *Life* magazines sat.

"You care about *him* so much," he said to her, his voice husky. "Why don't you just *go* with him!"

Andrew Snow lifted his head at that, but he didn't speak. I'd come up behind Rew and saw now that Gran's eyes were filling with tears.

"Rew . . ." I started.

He didn't let me finish. He kicked the side table hard, and the *Life* magazines toppled over. Gran and I both jumped, and Andrew Snow half rose, but Rew didn't care. He grabbed the magazines and threw them, threw them at Andrew Snow, one after the other. I saw Joe DiMaggio's face fly by, saw Andrew Snow duck. He walked across the room and grabbed Rew's wrist, pulling him to his feet before he could scoop up another magazine.

I ran at Andrew Snow then, taking hold of his arm and trying to get him to release Rew. Gran was on her feet.

"Let him go!" I yelled. "You'll break his arm!"

Andrew Snow abruptly let Rew loose, and Rew staggered backward.

"I wasn't hurting him," Andrew Snow said. "I was stopping him."

I ignored that. "You okay?" I asked Rew.

But he didn't answer. He just scooped one more magazine off the floor and threw it directly at Andrew Snow's face before he turned and dashed upstairs. A second later, he slammed his bedroom door so hard, the ceiling shook.

Gran hadn't moved. She just stood there, looking at the mess.

"I'll clean it up, Gran," I whispered to her, not wanting Andrew Snow to hear.

But he wasn't paying attention anyway. I stole a glance at him out of the corner of my eye, to see if he'd gone back to his chair, but he was looking at Gran, his face unreadable. I looked at Gran, too. Would he do something to her? Was *that* how bad he was? Did he think Gran could have stopped Rew? I wondered how well he really knew her. Or how well she knew him. Because Gran didn't seem scared when I turned to her. Just sad. Awfully sad.

Then Andrew Snow came up close to her, and he

whispered, too, but I could hear him anyway. And what he said surprised me, because it had nothing to do with Rew at all.

"What did you think would happen?" he asked Gran. "When you did this?"

I hadn't an idea in the world what he meant. But Gran must have, because she looked at him so suddenly, and with such a terrible sadness in her face, that I had to look away. I couldn't stand it. And then she went upstairs, too, and shut her door, but quietly.

Chapter 11

Gran stayed up in her room, refusing the food I brought her, her face to the wall. Rew came down, though. Around lunchtime he walked downstairs, making a point of turning his face from Andrew Snow, who sat with his chair tipped back against the front door, just staring up into nothing.

Rew and I poured cereal and milk for lunch. Rew liked cereal, but I rarely let him have it. Cereal boxes are bulky, and I hated carrying them home from the store. But when he came down now and pulled out the Super Sugar Crisp, I decided not to make an issue of it. So we sat there, eating cereal and stealing glances at Andrew Snow. He didn't bother us, but he looked our way plenty, an expression on his face that told me he wanted to say something. I guess Rew felt it, too, because he started in on Andrew Snow as soon as he'd finished his bowl. In fact, he spent a good half hour taunting him, promising he'd run at the first chance and get the police to put Andrew Snow back where he belonged.

Andrew Snow ignored him, and after a while, unable to listen anymore, I went upstairs and tried to make Gran talk to me, tried to get her to tell me something that made sense. But Gran said not a word.

And so finally I went back down to them. Andrew Snow sat in that chair by the door, face expressionless, watching Rew, watching me as I came down the stairs.

"You get years and years for holding people hostage," Rew was saying to him. "Maybe the death penalty, even."

Andrew Snow didn't answer.

"You'll fall asleep, you know," Rew said. "And then I'll do it. You can't stay awake forever."

Andrew Snow studied Rew, his lips pressed together in a line.

"How do you know I won't hurt someone once you're gone?" he said. "Don't you care at all about them?" He nodded toward me, and up in the direction of Gran's room.

Rew turned his face away.

Like those people in the embassy over in Iran, we were captives. Andrew Snow held us, with his grim face and his back to the door. If my figuring was right, then according to ABC, the hostages had been held for

243 days by the time we joined them, in our way. For us, day one was a Thursday. The third of July.

The heat of that day pressed itself through the windows, even after Andrew Snow had shut them. I went and stood by the kitchen door, looking out the back window at the Zebra Forest, thinking how it would be cool there now, in the shade. Thinking how if this were yesterday, I might be happy.

Someone came into the kitchen behind me. I thought it was Rew, but when I turned, I found Andrew Snow. He'd managed to chain the living-room door and wedge his chair against it so it would take a while to yank open.

"They'll come back for you," I said. "They don't just let people walk out of prison, you know."

Andrew Snow raised his eyebrows. "You know much about prisons?" he asked me.

I shrugged.

He pulled out a kitchen chair and sat down. Through the kitchen door, I could just see Rew on the stairs, listening, his face pale, his head resting against the rungs of the banister. I guessed all that yelling had tired him out.

"Then I'll tell you something," Andrew Snow said. "Policemen don't pay attention. They've checked their box. They've been here. They're done. They've got too many other things to worry about, specifically the forty-nine other guys that headed up that highway. I'm not worried."

He sounded like a liar, though. And not even a good one, like Gran.

So I said, "Yeah, well, you can't keep us here forever, you know. People will be looking."

He didn't answer right away. But he looked around the kitchen.

"You have many people here? Does your Gran have a lot of people?"

There was something funny in his voice when he said it.

I didn't know how to answer that, so I looked past him, wishing Rew had an answer. Andrew Snow turned and looked, too, at Rew on the stairs. Then he looked down at his hands and around our kitchen. He seemed to want to say something more but took a long time with it.

"They call her Morgan here?"

"What?"

"Miz Morgan. That's what they called her this morning. Is that her name here?"

He asked it soft, like a regular person would. I nodded.

"You too?"

"Just at school," I said, unsure whether I should tell him anything. Not knowing what he meant to do. "It's for her mother."

But he didn't do anything that I could see except look confused. "Her mother?" he asked.

It was strange, having a conversation with him, this man who'd so lately dragged me downstairs and nearly smothered me. But I couldn't see any way out of it, so I said, "That was her last name. Her mother, from Chicago."

But that wasn't what he'd been after, because he sat up in the chair then, looking annoyed. "I know that. Don't you think I know that? I spent summers with my grandmother Morgan."

His grandmother Morgan. I'd never thought of it that way. For a minute, I caught myself wanting to ask him something. Ask him what it had been like in that apartment building, with all the cousins and the shop downstairs. But I clamped my mouth shut before I did. I didn't think I ought to get too friendly, knowing what I did about him. So I said nothing.

Finally, he said, "Did your Gran ever talk about me?"

I was so startled by the question that I just gaped at him for a minute. Then I shook my head.

"She said you were dead," I said. "A long time ago."

Rew had been listening. He'd gotten up from the

stairs so quietly, I hadn't noticed him until he was standing just outside the kitchen door.

"You should be dead," he said. "I wish you were."

Andrew Snow didn't look at him right away. But I saw his mouth go tight and a muscle jump in his jaw. He stared straight ahead for a minute before turning slowly to look at Rew.

"Well, I'm not dead," he said in a low voice. "I'm here now. Alive. And I'm staying."

Rew flushed. "I hate you," he said, his voice shaking. "All of us do. Even your own mother wishes you were dead."

He rushed upstairs then, and when he'd gone, Andrew Snow dropped his head into his hands.

For a second, I felt bad at what Rew had said. If I hadn't known what Andrew Snow had done, I'd have thought maybe he cared that Rew said that. And besides, I didn't think it was true. Gran didn't hate Andrew Snow. At least I didn't think so. But then, maybe I didn't know much about Gran after all.

Chapter 12

That night, I went upstairs to Rew and found him sitting cross-legged on his bed, writing something in one of the spiral-bound notebooks he had from school.

He'd refused dinner, and Gran hadn't come down, so I had eaten a silent supper of leftovers, hastily, at the kitchen table. Andrew Snow asked me for something to eat, too, and even though I wanted to refuse, I didn't think I ought to. So I made him a sandwich, and took it to him at the door.

"It's just peanut butter and jelly," I told him. "If you want something better, you can get it yourself, I guess."

He picked it up and seemed to inspect it. "No," he said. "This'll be fine."

I walked away from him then, to make Rew something. But from the kitchen, I heard him again. "It's good," he said. "Thank you."

I made Rew's sandwich, an extra thick one, and took it up to him with some orange juice in a glass, the way we sometimes did on Mother's Day for Gran.

He looked up at me when I came in and surprised me by looking almost happy.

"What're you doing?" I asked him. I set the tray down on his bookcase and went over to his bed. "Drawing?"

He finished whatever he'd been writing, ripped the paper neatly from the notebook, and handed it over to me. In big letters, he'd written, "Please help us. We live at 6 Willow Road, at the far end. A man from the prison is holding us HOSTAGE. Please HELP!"

My stomach jumped a little when I read it.

"What are you going to do with it?" I asked him. "It's not like someone's coming here to get it."

The mailman never came to our house. When we'd first moved, Gran had gone into town and set up a post-office box, which is a tiny cabinet where they put your mail over at the post office, and you go and pick it up with a little key. Once, in the third grade, our teacher had wanted us all to write our addresses down so we could have pen pals — other kids we wrote to some-where in a faraway country. But Gran didn't like that one bit. She told me then to tell the teacher we didn't give our address out, and that if she needed me to write a letter, I could write one to Beth, to her house in town. Of course,

I didn't tell the teacher this. I just pretended like I forgot about the assignment, and she let it go.

But that was when I learned about the post office, and boxes. And then a while later, when it got too hard for Gran to go into town to get the bills, she taught me how to use it. Our box was registered under the name Morgan, and it came with a number, and that funny-size key. Every few weeks, I'd go to the post office and empty it, and that was enough, because all that ever came there were bills, anyway; we never got any letters.

So we didn't have any cheerful mailman coming to our door each day. And he was probably happy about it, since we didn't live near anybody anyway. Which is why I thought Rew had gone off the deep end, writing that letter.

"We're not going anywhere," I said to him again. "You have as good a chance of sending the police a letter as you do of calling them on the phone." Andrew Snow had been sure to rip the cord out of the phone, in case we got any ideas about using it while he was sleeping or in the bathroom.

But Rew shook his head, excited. "Look," he said, and he pulled an envelope out from under the notebook. In big letters across the front, he'd written "Police Chief, Sunshine" as neatly as he could.

"So?" I asked him.

"So you wait, Annie. You'll see," he said to me. "You think he can keep the house shut up like this forever? In a few days, we're going to need food, you know. What will he do then? I'll tell you — he's going to send someone."

I just looked at him, not understanding, and he jumped up onto his knees, leaning toward me to explain it, he was so wound up.

"It's gonna be *you*, don't you see? He can't send Gran, and he *won't* send me. He'll send you — just like Gran does! And when you go, you'll put this right in the mail, and he'll never know you did it! See? Then you'll come back, and he'll think it's all just fine, that he's got us, but a day later — *pow!* — here they come!"

I didn't like it. I wanted to be free of Andrew Snow, all right, but Rew's letter made me uneasy. What would Gran think of it?

"I don't know," I told him. "What if they come and start shooting or something? We could get hurt. And Gran — well, you saw what she did when they came. She was scared they'd hurt him."

Rew let out a little puff of exasperation. "They won't! Don't worry! Nothing's going to happen. They'll just get him and take him away."

"I don't know," I said again. "Accidents happen. Remember those people that got killed in the spring, trying to rescue those guys in Iran?" I had seen that on ABC, at Beth's.

"All *right,*" Rew said, annoyed. He pulled the letter back from me, picked up his pen, and added another line to his note. Then he shoved it back into my hand. He had added, "And please no shooting" at the bottom and underlined it.

"Okay?" he said.

Still, I didn't want to take the letter. So I said, "You don't have the right address, anyway. You can't just address something 'Police Chief.' That's like kids writing to Santa Claus at the North Pole."

Rew shook his head. "It's not," he told me. "It's more like calling the operator in an emergency. I'll put this on it, see?" He took out a red marker and wrote EMER-GENCY across the front of the envelope.

I looked at it, dismayed.

But Rew was happier than ever. "Get some stamps," he told me, excited now. I kept the stamps in my room, because I was the one who sent out the bills most of the time. And, watching Rew move with such agitation, I knew I didn't have much choice. So I got him one.

He stamped and sealed his letter and then explained his plan again. "Gran won't know, and neither will *he,*" he told me. "They'll just think they found him out of luck, you know? But they'll get him, and that's the point."

The more I thought about it, the less I liked it.

"He'll go away soon enough," I told him. "I don't think this is such a good idea. What if they come and see Gran and think she's too sick to be with us anymore? Then what's going to happen? We'll have more than Adele Parks coming here then!"

But Rew wouldn't have it. He moved around the room, so jumpy, I was put in mind of Mrs. Roberts telling the boys to settle down 'cause they had "ants in their pants."

"That won't happen," he said, real fast. "They'll see that *he* did that. She'll get better once they take him, anyway. You'll see."

I didn't think so, but I could tell when there was no talking to Rew. He didn't act angry anymore, exactly, but I had a feeling that his chess mind wasn't working just then. "Promise me," he said, pushing the letter into my hands. "Promise me you'll do it."

"But, Rew—" I began, and then he did get mad, a flash of fury reddening his face.

"Whose side are you on, anyway?" he asked me, in a whisper that sounded more like a shout. "Are you on *his* now?"

I shook my head. "No, but—" But there was no but, and so I reluctantly took the letter.

"Okay," I said. "I'll do it." And I slipped it into my pocket.

"Promise?" he asked again.

I didn't want to promise, but there was nothing else to say.

"Yeah," I said at last. "I promise."

Chapter 13

After my promise, Rew's appetite returned. He ate the sandwich I had brought him and drank the juice. Then he pulled *Treasure Island* back into his lap and rubbed his hand over the old pages.

"They don't get him in the end because he's too smart," he said, grinning suddenly, and I knew he meant Long John Silver. "No one can keep hold of him."

He was back to our old argument about whether the double-crossing pirate was the best or worst person in the story.

We both liked Jim, because after all, he was good. "*And* he keeps the treasure" was how I'd always argue it. But that was where our agreement ended.

From there, I'd take up for my particular favorite — Dr. Livesey — who helps Jim right from the start. The doctor isn't afraid of anybody, ever. I had a list of the doctor's strengths, which I'd tick off for Rew when he told me that Dr. Livesey was okay but boring.

For one, the doctor never yelled at anyone, like that old squire or the captain. He only fought when he had to, and he stuck it out the whole trip, never ran off, and even took care of the pirates some.

It was a secret of mine that even though we agreed on liking Jim, it practically killed me that our hero ran off out of the stockade, leaving all his friends and never telling Dr. Livesey a thing about it. When we talked about it, Rew said that was okay, because didn't Jim get the ship for them afterward? Didn't it end up saving them? I knew it did, but somehow, it just didn't seem right. And then, I'd always argue, it was the doctor who saved Jim and old Long John in the end. "Long John Silver himself said it," I would tell him, quoting the pirate in the raspy voice I imagined would have been the sound of Long John Silver: "'Thank ye kindly, doctor. . . . You came in in about the nick, I guess, for me and Hawkins.'"

"Sure," Rew would say. "But he *had* to say that. If you want to look at it that way, then it was Ben Gunn who saved them, really." We both always laughed at that, because Ben Gunn, the crazy man who'd been marooned on the island, wasn't anybody's favorite.

We'd spend at least an hour a week on this topic in

the Zebra, and it was a kind of joke we had, going back over it, deciding whether we were happy or not that Long John Silver got his one measly bag of coins and escaped at the end.

It seemed to me that after writing his letter, Rew felt we were almost as good as free. Maybe that's why he'd started our game up again. So I said what I always said when we talked about Long John Silver: "Well, he only got that one bag of coins, anyway. And only 'cause Ben Gunn let him. He couldn't have lived long on that."

Rew lay back on his bed and glanced out the window. It was getting dark now, the sky going purple over the Zebra. I guess he realized then that even if Andrew Snow did send me out and I mailed his letter, we wouldn't be free for a while. Rew's realistic that way. He frowned, lying there, and pulled his book up near his face, breathing in the smell of it. It was an old book, and beat up, but it had the good, sweet aroma of old paper. Books have that, I've noticed. If they don't get moldy, they're nice. We had our share of moldy books down in the cellar. But *Treasure Island* still had that nice old library smell to it. He kept his face in there so long, I got nervous he might cry again. But he didn't. After a while, he closed the book and rested his head on it, looking tired.

"If there were a tree outside my window, we wouldn't need to send the letter," he said quietly. "I'd just climb down it and run to the police, and he'd never even know it. I'd do it in the night."

"You wouldn't," I said. "You'd never find the way in the dark, so far from town. You'd get hit by a car or something first."

"I wouldn't," he said. "I could do it. I'd do it in the day, even, if I didn't think he'd hurt you and Gran."

In a funny way, I felt happy all of a sudden, hearing him include Gran. Rew could get really mad, but he never stayed angry at me or Gran too long.

I looked down at the faded pattern of his quilt, a mishmash of cowboys and spaceships and any boy thing Gran could find. She'd made it for him when he was just born, she told him once, as a birthday gift. According to Gran, I'd had one, too, once upon a time, with princesses and ribbons on it. But in a fit of temper when I was two, my mother had thrown it in the trash.

"You think he'd do that?" I asked him. "Hurt us? Really?"

"He's mean enough to," Rew said. "Didn't you think so when he pulled us down the stairs that way? He's crazy, Annie. He's bad."

I thought about it. Andrew Snow was strong — that was certain. He'd held me and Rew each with just the one hand. And when those policemen had come, he hadn't hesitated a second. But then, he hadn't exactly hurt us, either. And he'd thanked me for making him a sandwich. Did bad people say thank you? I thought of the letter then, sitting in my pocket. I wished I didn't have it.

"He killed someone," Rew said, reading my thoughts.

Rew knew things, better than me usually. But it was hard to picture the man who had put his head in his hands doing something like that. In my mind, I tried to make a story about it so I could understand it better. But the story wouldn't come.

I sat with Rew until he fell asleep and then made my way downstairs. Andrew Snow was sitting in the chair by the door, looking out at the night. From that window, you could just see the edge of the Zebra.

I'd been outside in the dark lots of times, and I loved the Zebra in moonlight. We never went far into it at night, but sometimes in winter, Rew and I went out all bundled up and just sat at the edge there, watching the clean, star-pricked sky rise up over all those trees. I thought about Andrew Snow wandering through it in the dark. I didn't think he would have noticed the sky.

He looked a little surprised to see me standing there so long, just looking. Maybe he thought I wanted him to say something. So he did.

"You're eleven, aren't you?" he said to me.

I nodded.

"I remember you as a tiny thing," he said. "Last time

I saw you, you were just three. But you talked then. Did your Gran ever tell you?"

I shook my head. "She doesn't tell about those times," I said. "She doesn't like to remember them."

He stared at me then, as if he expected me to say something more. But I didn't.

"I thought maybe you'd have asked her," he said at last. "You might have wanted to know."

Sometimes lying is so easy, you do it before you even think.

"No," I said. "I never did."

Chapter 14

Being a hostage wasn't anything like I imagined it would be, having heard about it from the news on ABC. I had never imagined hostages eating, for example. I'd never wondered how they slept at night.

But all those things occurred to me on day two of our captivity. They came up because Andrew Snow went into our kitchen.

Overnight he had found an even better way to chain the front door shut, so we couldn't get outside. That left him free to explore a little, and the first thing he did was look in our cabinets.

There wasn't much inside. After our dinner party the night before he came, there were few groceries left, considering we usually weren't too well stocked anyway. He poked around, then asked me what we usually ate.

I shrugged, mindful of Rew, seething in the front room, listening to me converse with the enemy.

"I mean when your Gran cooks for you," he prompted.

I tried to come up with an answer that wouldn't hurt Gran or enrage Rew.

"She doesn't cook that much," I said carefully. "But we get by."

Andrew Snow looked at me. "Who does the shopping?" he asked.

It took a minute for me to answer him, I was so struck by how Rew had known he'd be asking that. My brother was too smart for himself, I thought. In a way, it scared me. Andrew Snow was waiting for an answer, though, so I said, "Sometimes Gran, sometimes me."

"You?"

"I can do it," I said, indignant. "If she gives me a list, and money."

"Well," he said, looking again at the nearly empty cupboard, "I can give you a list. But what about money? Is there some in the house here?"

"Just a little," I said, careful, in case he meant to trick me. "Just enough for food and stuff."

Andrew Snow tilted his head and sighed. It startled me, because Rew does that, too, sometimes, when he gets tired. "I'm not going to take it," he said, "if that's what you're thinking. But we will need to eat."

He left me then and went through the front room

and up the stairs. I didn't understand what he meant to do until it was too late, when I heard him knocking on Gran's door.

I dashed after him then.

"Leave her be!" I said, and Rew, who had followed me up, pushed him from behind. But Andrew Snow paid no attention.

"Mom," he said. The word was so strange, it stopped us both for a moment. Of course, he must have called her that once.

"Open up. I want to talk to you."

I could hear the bed creak on the other side of the door. Gran didn't answer.

Andrew Snow looked over his shoulder at us. "Go downstairs," he said. "I only want to talk to her."

Neither of us moved. He put his hand on the doorknob. The door opened easily. Gran never locked it. She didn't have to. We knew when to leave her be.

Gran was lying in her bed, her back to us, her face to the wall. I knew she was awake. When she heard the door open, she shook her head ever so slightly.

Andrew Snow stiffened. "I need to talk to you," he said again, louder this time.

When Gran didn't move, he said, "You can't turn your back forever, Mom. Not anymore. I'll get an answer.

You owe me that. And this time, it will be more than twenty words."

Gran shook her head again, and one hand came up over her ear.

"Leave her be," I whispered to Andrew Snow. "Please just let her alone."

Andrew Snow didn't answer me, but he stood there, his hand so white on the doorknob that I took a step back, sure he was going to slam it. But he only held it there for another minute. Then he shook his head, sighed, and closed the door.

Chapter 15

The next day, after checking that all the doors and windows were secured, Andrew Snow left us downstairs alone while he took a shower. The minute he heard the water run, Rew, who'd been slumping on the stairs, unraveling part of the old carpet that padded the steps, took off for the kitchen. I followed him and found him yanking open drawers, rifling through them, and then slamming them shut.

"What are you looking for?" I asked him. "You saw him take the key."

Scraps of paper, pens, and the occasional bottle cap went flying as he dug around.

"Something," he said. "Anything. He thinks we're helpless. We can't do anything. Well, he doesn't *know* us."

I didn't see what pawing through the kitchen drawers was going to get us. I started to tell him the project was hopeless, but he ignored me. Finally, he let out a happy little cry and pulled out the one sharp thing in the kitchen, a long paring knife we used to cut vegetables, when we had them.

"Rew," I said.

He grinned and ran over to the kitchen door, jabbing the knife tip into the lock. He jiggled it, shoved it in deeper, and twisted it again. He grimaced with the effort of it, closing his eyes as he worked the knife into the lock. Nothing clicked. He pulled it out to find the knife tip bent at a new angle.

"Stupid knife," he said, pressing it on the counter and trying to force it back into shape. He grunted with the effort.

I'd pulled out a kitchen chair to watch him work, but now I got up to see if I could help. A sound from the living room made us turn.

Andrew Snow, hair dripping, was standing in the kitchen doorway. His eyes darted to the knife in Rew's hand, and he lunged across the room so fast neither of us had time to react. His fingers clamped round Rew's wrist, and he shook it once, hard. The knife clattered to the floor.

Andrew Snow bent swiftly and pocketed it. When he looked up again, his face was as blotchy as Rew's. He advanced on my brother, and I pushed my way in between them, just in case. Through his wet, smelly shirt, I could see his chest heaving, but when he spoke, it was almost a whisper.

"You know what it is to cut someone? You know what that's like?" he asked. His eyes were so wide open, I had to look away. "You want to see someone's blood come?"

Behind me I could hear Rew breathing heavy.

"You think about that," Andrew Snow said. "You think if that's something you want to see now."

I wanted to run, but I turned to see Rew staring straight ahead, quaking with outrage. He looked like he'd swallowed something rotten, and he pulled away from us both, pushing past Andrew Snow and stomping toward the living room.

At the door, he turned, face blazing.

"You think I'd be like you?" Rew spat. "Is that what you think? I'd rather *die* than be like you."

Then he spun around and ran upstairs.

I stood, my back pressed against the counter, Andrew Snow still too close to me, half turned as he watched Rew go. He stood rigid, unmoving except for his hands, which were balled into fists so tight they shook.

"He was only trying to pick the lock," I said quietly. "He wasn't going to hurt you."

Andrew Snow didn't look at me. He stood like that, too still, until I'd slipped past him and fled the kitchen.

Chapter 16

On the fifth day of our captivity, a Monday, Rew's prediction came true. Andrew Snow sent me on a supply run.

He'd been careful with the list. Unlike Gran's lists, which consisted of anything she felt like that day, sometimes strange things, like peaches and avocados, sometimes chocolate or condensed milk, Andrew Snow's list was methodical. It had all the food groups, including vegetables. Plus, he wanted a newspaper.

I dug the money out of one of Gran's hiding places — a fake book that was really a box she kept in the bookcase. One of the jobs I'd gotten in the last year was doing Gran's banking, which meant going to town and taking out the money we needed for the month. At the bank, Gran kept all the money the insurance company had given her after Grandpa Snow died, and to get some of it, I'd bring her withdrawal slip all filled out, and then go round the house with the fresh bills, filling up her several hiding places. The fake book was my favorite, and so I put twenties in there, because I used twenties at the grocery. I didn't know how that book was meant to fool anyone, since it was unlike any other we had. Our house was a paperback house, and filled with magazines. The fake book looked like it had been made of leather and had gold lettering on it, even though it was nothing more than painted cardboard. Rew always said it was stupid to put money in a book with gold lettering, but I didn't think crooks were smart enough to think of that, so I kept right on doing it. This time, though, with Andrew Snow in the house, I did regret it. Still, I tried to take the cash out while he was in the bathroom. It didn't work. He came out just as I was slipping the book back into the shelf.

"I know about it already," he said when he saw me shove it back quick, trying to pretend it was nothing. "She's always had it. Drove my father crazy, but she used to say that if ever there was a hurricane, or a war or something, one should have cash on hand." I felt stupid then, and something else, too. I guess it was knowing then that no matter how much I wished he weren't, this was the real Andrew Snow. Maybe up till then I thought Gran might have made a mistake. Maybe this red-haired man wasn't our father. But he was. I knew it because Gran had said that same thing to us, about hurricanes and wars. She'd said it a million times.

All of a sudden, I could have cried. My throat hurt and my eyes got hot, and if it had been any other day, I would have sat down on the couch and just done it. But Andrew Snow would have seen me, so I bit my lip instead, folded the money, put it into my pocket, and walked to the door.

"Do you want me to go or not?" I asked him.

Just then Rew came running down the stairs. He stopped short at the bottom.

Andrew Snow looked at him. "You're not going," he said, and his voice had that edge to it again. "Just your sister."

"I know that," Rew said, sounding mad. But when Andrew Snow turned back to me, Rew gave me a nod and patted his pocket, raising his eyebrows to make sure I had the letter with me. I didn't do anything in response; Andrew Snow was looking right at me, after all.

Andrew Snow walked over and fiddled with the chains he'd rigged up. But just as he got ready to open the door, he gave me a sharp last look.

"Before you think of saying anything, remember I have them right here with me," he said.

I looked past him at Rew, who gave me an encouraging smile.

I didn't need to be reminded.

Chapter 17

Outside, I could smell the Zebra. Even if for some reason I stopped feeling cold or hot or rain or sun, I bet I could close my eyes and still tell which season I was in just by the smell of the trees and dirt there. Spring was sweet mud and flowers. Fall had a kind of moldy edge to it, and winter was all dust and bark. As for summer, the Zebra carried a mossy, thick aroma full of baking leaves and oozing sap, which I guess was its growing smell.

If Andrew Snow hadn't been watching me from the window, I'd have veered off and run straight for it, just to breathe it in for a while. But he was, so I forced myself to turn my back and walk the quarter mile out to the bus. I waited on the main road, baking in the heat, until it came. I didn't mind taking the bus alone, and I didn't mind the shopping, but that morning, on my own for the first time in five days, I felt sick at the thought of seeing other people. It felt as if the skin on my head had shrunk and now stretched tight across my skull, trying to squeeze my brains.

Somehow, they'd know. Just by looking at me, they'd figure it out. And then they'd go back to the house, and no matter what Rew said, it would be the police and maybe even the SWAT team, and they'd barge right in. They'd break the door down, and they'd shoot Andrew Snow, and maybe Gran and Rew, just by accident. I shuddered, standing there, imagining it. And I caught myself trying to picture what Andrew Snow would do, what he'd think when they came. *She told.* That's what he'd think. And he'd be mad. He'd be so mad. And then they'd shoot him.

But when the bus pulled up ten minutes later and I got on and paid my fare, no one even looked my way. I knew the bus driver on that route, and he gave me his usual little smile when I passed. I didn't say anything, and he didn't, either. Sometimes I'd know someone on the bus, one of the people riding. But not this day. And no one said a thing to me, and I got off in town like I would have on any regular day.

The nearest mailbox was just by the bus stop, and I couldn't help but pass it when I got off at my stop. Rew's letter was in my pocket, all right, and it kind of amazed me that I still had it. If Andrew Snow had really been like Rew, he'd have searched me before I left. He'd have thought of something like this. But maybe that kind of thinking came from our mother. I didn't know.

A couple of people had gotten off the bus with me, and I wasn't planning on taking the letter out in front of any of them, so I stood there, looking up at the sky, pretending I'd forgotten something on my grocery list and just generally looking kind of blank, until they'd wandered off. Then I pulled the letter from my pocket.

Rew's big, careful writing and that red EMERGENCY made my heart jump. I didn't like to look at it. I thought of shoving it fast, into the box, and walking off quick the other way. When did they pick up the mail, anyway? When would they get it? Probably not until the afternoon. And then it would take a day or so in the mail. Which meant that the police chief wouldn't get it and come running until at least Thursday or so. Andrew Snow would be there all that time, watching me. And he'd probably figure out what I'd done. He'd know it for sure when they came.

I looked again at the letter. Maybe he would just go away on his own. Maybe he would go tomorrow. He'd go to Mexico or Canada or wherever, and we wouldn't see him anymore. And no police would come to our house, either.

Rew was smart, but he was impatient, too. We could wait a while longer. It wouldn't hurt us too much. So I put the letter back in my pocket. I'd have time to mail it later if I needed to.

Chapter 18

Since my first time with Rew at the big grocery store, I didn't go to that one anymore. Instead I'd found a little market downtown, near the post office and the bank, and I went there. It stood on the corner, next to the drugstore, with those dark, painted windows that reflect back at you on the outside and the words SUN-SHINE GROCERY in half-lit letters across the top.

Sunshine Grocery looked shabby, but I had picked it out of the several smaller area markets for two reasons, both of which had to do with Molly, the young woman who sat behind the counter. First, Molly was a fanatic TV watcher, and she kept a little set behind the counter going full-time. So I'd go in there to shop and get to hear on *Phil Donahue* why Farrah Fawcett left *Charlie's Angels* after just one season.

The other thing I loved about Molly was her talent at gum chewing. When I first found Sunshine Grocery, it was the gum popping that brought me back. Molly must have been about twenty years old, and she worked the counter alone for most of the day. I took an interest in everything about her. So did Beth, who sometimes came with me when I went shopping on school days.

For someone who worked in a food store all day, Molly didn't seem like she ate much. She had a narrow, pointy face, made pointier by the way she wore her hair. It was twice as wide as her face, blown back in soft brown wings and separated by the most perfect part anyone had ever seen. It was the kind you make with the end of a comb when your hair's still wet, or at least that's what Beth had figured out once she tried it. Just before Molly would pop a bubble, she'd flip her head to make her hair whip back, out of the way. And then she'd blow a huge one, let it hang for a second, and snap it right back. She never got any on her face, either.

I could blow a bubble, at least a small one, but I could not pop my gum like that. One day after school when I first found the market, I'd taken Beth with me, and the two of us loitered by the fresh-fruit bins, studying Molly a long time, watching her work that gum. Then we'd bought a pack each, taken it out to the sidewalk around the corner from the bank, and spent half an hour trying to get a nice-sounding crack out of our wads. But all we did was spit at each other a lot.

Standing outside the grocery that morning, I suddenly missed Beth so bad I almost had to sit down. If she were next to me, we could pretend to be talking to each other when we went in, and no one would notice anything different. Nobody would look too close or wonder about why I had a different list today, why I suddenly had an interest in bringing home a newspaper. But then, if Beth were around, what would I have said about Andrew Snow? It was all too confusing. I shook my head and forced myself to push open the door, making the bell ping.

Glancing down at my hands, I willed them not to shake when the time came to hand Molly the money. Wasn't I supposed to be a good liar? The TV was on, of course, but Molly had it low. She wasn't watching it — she was reading the paper, which was a sight in itself. She was still chewing, though, faster than ever, and I could smell Bubblicious just as soon as I came in. Molly looked up, nodded at me, and went back to her paper. It was the local news, and she was shaking her head over it. I went around collecting the things on Andrew Snow's list, trying to figure out where some of the new ones — like celery and kidney beans — were to be found, when I heard the bell ping again.

I took longer than usual to get back to the front with my things, and I dragged my feet a little, too, worrying about Molly noticing my list. Molly didn't know a thing about my fascination with her, but she was friendly and always made a point of saying something to me when I came to the counter. Since she knew practically nothing about me, it usually had to do with what I was buying. If I got us ice cream, for example, she'd say, "Having a party?" or when I got cough syrup, because Rew had a cold, she'd ask me who was sick.

Turned out I didn't have to worry today, though, because when I got up toward the front, where I could hear that familiar snap of gum, I found another woman there as well, leaning over the paper on the counter and shaking her head.

"Art Belmont's already been put on notice," the woman was saying. "And John Townson, too. It's an awful thing."

Molly shook her head. "Well, so many escape, you can't expect them to do nothing, I guess."

The other woman snorted. "They could dock their pay, I expect! They don't have to *fire* them! People have to make a living! And it wasn't as if five men at the front could stop a riot. What did they expect them to do, anyway? Scapegoats, that's what they are. That prison was always understaffed. So what do they do? Give people the boot!"

I don't think it occurred to me till then that the Enderfield where everybody worked was the same place Andrew Snow had lived so many years. It was hard to put it together, somehow. But suddenly I did see, listening there in the grocery, that there were people in town — people I might have seen before — who would recognize Andrew Snow. If he ever did come out of our house and tried walking the streets of Sunshine, they'd know him. He couldn't even walk into town to take the Trailways bus. He'd get caught, if he did that, even in regular clothes. I wondered why I didn't feel good, thinking that right then. It was certainly something to tell Rew. He'd be happy. And I guess I was, too. But right then I just felt irritated. Maybe because it was hot and I didn't like buying strange groceries that took too long to find.

Molly meanwhile was nodding wisely and chewing some more. "Maybe they'll let it go," she said. "If they round them all up, maybe they'll settle down."

The woman I didn't know shook her head and tapped the paper. "See here? They've gotten about eight of them, that's all. Eight out of something like *forty-eight*. No, more of those guys will be fired. I just hope it isn't Sammy. His wife's expecting."

Molly snapped her gum and shook her head. "Where'd they all go? It does make me awful uneasy — all those murderers and criminals running round the area."

"Who knows, by now?" the other woman said. "I heard a couple of them got picked up at the bus station in the next town, and one at a girlfriend's house. Then there were four idiots who had the bad luck to try to take a van from a couple of off-duty state troopers. But the others, they scattered. They're probably all in Washington, D.C., by now. Or maybe even halfway to New York. Don't you worry about seeing them in Sunshine. They're all a hundred miles up the road. Didn't the police come to your door the other day, checking?"

"Yeah," Molly said. "You're right. But it'll hurt people round here just the same. I wonder how many more will be looking for work by next week."

I slipped round the woman and put a copy of the paper in with my groceries, heart beating faster as I did it. Then I took a step back and cleared my throat. Molly looked up. "Oh, here you go, Annie. You want to check out?"

I nodded. Molly swept aside her paper, and the woman moved on into the store, pushing her cart.

"At least there's some news around here, right?" she said to me. Then she noticed my paper. To my relief, she only smiled.

"Guess everyone's reading the reports now, aren't they?"

"Yeah," I said. "It's for my gran."

She patted my hand as I laid the vegetables on the counter.

"Well, you tell her not to get too worked up about it," she said. "Things'll settle down quick enough."

I tried to nod, afraid to meet her eye. Instead, I motioned toward the bottom half of her paper.

"I've been wondering about those hostages," I said.

"Oh, them," she said. "Yeah, they're still there. Those awful Iranians. Somebody ought to bomb them."

"But what about the Americans? They'd still be in there."

"Oh, yeah," she said, snapping her gum again. "I meant after they got 'em out."

She gave me my change then. "No gum today?" she asked. But I shook my head. I wasn't in the mood for gum just then.

Chapter 19

When I got back home, I had to wait outside, knocking, until Andrew Snow unchained the door and let me in.

"What took so long?" I asked Rew after Andrew Snow had rebolted the door and taken the groceries into the kitchen without a word. Rew had been on the stairs with his *Treasure Island*. He didn't seem to read it so much now as just hold it. Whenever Andrew Snow passed by, he'd pull the book up to his chest, as if to hide it.

Rew acted like he hadn't even heard my question. "Did you do it?" he asked me eagerly.

I wanted to tell him the truth. I really did. But something in his face, so intense, so set, stopped me. And so I did something I never had before. I lied to Rew.

"Yeah," I said. "I did it."

His face shone, but I felt like I might throw up. I'd never broken a promise to him before. I didn't want him to talk about it anymore, so I asked again, "What took him so long to open the door?"

Rew didn't even seem to notice how upset I was, he was so keyed up. "He was up there again, trying to get her to talk," he told me. "Only he didn't open the door this time."

"What does he want from her?" I said. "What does he care, anyway? He wasn't looking for us. It's not like he meant to find us."

"I can't wait until he's gone," Rew said, bouncing a little in anticipation. "I wish he'd leave right now. But anyway, when they come, they'll get him. Then they'll lock him back up forever."

Andrew Snow came out of the kitchen before I could answer, the newspaper in his hand. But instead of talking about it, he looked my way.

"You should take a drink," he said to me. "It's hot work, carrying those groceries all this way."

"I'm not thirsty," I said, even though I was.

"Well," Andrew Snow said, "it's up to you. At least we'll have supper tonight. And lunch tomorrow."

I just looked at him. He sat down in his chair by the door and bent over the paper. Rew's mood soured again the minute Andrew Snow walked into the room, and now he returned to the stairs, turned his back on Andrew Snow, and opened *Treasure Island* at random. I plopped myself down on the couch.

When we'd first started reading about Jim Hawkins, we'd sit in the living room and try to get the accents right, reading the story out loud and calling each other "matey" and "lad." But it turned out to be another of Gran's peculiarities that she didn't like to hear us reading *Treasure Island* out loud. One evening, she'd come downstairs unexpectedly and heard us at it. It was right at the best part, when Long John's leading Jim by a rope, holding it in his teeth, and he and the other pirates are climbing the hill on Treasure Island, trying to find the tall tree and the other signs that will lead them to the treasure. They don't know yet that it's gone because crazy Ben Gunn, who was marooned on the island three years earlier by the awful Captain Flint, already dug it up before they got there and hid it in his cave. While they're going up there, they start to hear a voice singing the old pirate song:

Fifteen men on the dead man's chest —
Yo-ho-ho, and a bottle of rum!

And they all go crazy, scared half to death thinking it's the spirit of the terrible Captain Flint, who killed his six companions so they wouldn't get at his treasure.

I love that part because all the time it's really just

Ben Gunn, trying to scare them away. Rew and I used to laugh our heads off when we read it. Sometimes we'd read it over again because the first time through, we laughed so hard, we missed parts.

But when Gran came down and heard us, she didn't think it was funny at all. She'd been smiling when she came downstairs, maybe hearing us laughing and wondering why, but when she realized what we were reading, the smile just dropped right off her face.

"What's wrong?" Rew asked her. And she looked at us funny but didn't answer right away. Finally, she said, "Nothing's wrong. But I don't know what you like in that book so much. It's all filled with misery. Barely any of the ones who sail make it home alive."

I thought this was the strangest way to look at *Treasure Island* I ever heard.

"But, Gran," I said, "it's just a story. And all the people you *like* in it get out. Jim, and the doctor, and the squire and them. Even Long John Silver!"

But Gran wouldn't have it. She said, "What about that poor boy Dick, who reads the Bible? They leave him there. And what about Ben Gunn?"

"Ben Gunn? He gets out, Gran! He even gets treasure!" Rew said.

But there was no arguing with her, and that was back when we still tried, so we took *Treasure Island* and went out to the Zebra to read it stretched out with our heads against a moss-padded root or with our backs against the trunks in a spot where the trees crowded so close you thought they were leaning in to hear the next chapter.

"She sure knows the story, though," Rew said when we were by ourselves under the trees. "I hardly remember Dick."

"But she forgot about Ben Gunn," I said. "They don't leave *him* on the island."

"Yeah," Rew said. "She forgot that part."

Sitting on the couch, with Rew curled on the stairs and Andrew Snow standing guard, I wished we could take the book and head outside, far out into the trees where we couldn't see the house anymore, to the places we knew where you could get so drowsy and relaxed on a summer afternoon, you'd fall asleep without knowing it and wake up only when the sun shifted through the leaves. I guess I was wishing so hard that I opened my mouth without thinking first.

"Hey, Rew," I said, trying to keep my voice low. "Want to go upstairs and read *Treasure Island* together?"

Rew didn't look too sure, but Andrew Snow didn't give him much chance to answer anyway, because he heard me. In a voice that sounded oddly pleased, he said, "Is that what you two do all day? Read?"

I didn't know how he meant that, so I half shrugged

and picked up one of Gran's magazines. It turned out to be the one from May 1949 where they had a picture of Franklin Delano Roosevelt as a toddler on the front cover. He was all dolled up, with long curls and even a dress. Gran had told us that's how they dressed rich little boys in the old days, but that only made it more funny, especially to Rew. I wanted to call him over and show it to him, but not with Andrew Snow there. So I put it back in the pile.

After a while, Andrew Snow broke the silence again.

"Because I notice you don't have a TV," he said, as if I'd been in a conversation with him, as if the room weren't dead silent unless he talked.

"So?" I said, not knowing what he wanted, really.

"So I guess you read, then," he said. "And play outside?"

Andrew Snow was, I was beginning to see, as peculiar as Gran. Did he care that we played outside? I wondered suddenly if he wasn't bored, too, maybe so bored he'd open the door and let us out. For some reason, I wanted suddenly to tell him about the Zebra, how in early spring, new oak leaves hung like tassels from the edge of each branch, so bright that when Rew had seen them once at dawn, he'd sworn they could glow in the dark. But then I thought better of it. It wasn't his business, anyway. That's what Rew would say.

When I didn't answer, he shifted his attention to Rew.

"I read *Treasure Island* when I was a kid," he said. "It was one of my favorites. Your gran got it for me."

Rew stiffened.

I thought I might not have heard him right. And it must have been that I had such a habit of talking it over with Rew that before I could stop myself, I asked, "What part did you like best?"

Andrew Snow looked over at me, and he seemed almost happy, maybe because I didn't ignore him. He said, "I like all the parts. The end, of course. Some people say it starts kind of slow, but I never thought so. I always liked that beginning, at the Admiral Benbow."

I wasn't about to tell him I didn't know what he was talking about. And when I sneaked a glance at Rew, I saw him holding himself as still as a statue. Then he saw me looking at him, and without a word, he went upstairs.

Chapter 20

Sometimes in those early days with Andrew Snow, I'd sit on the couch, trying to imagine the Americans in Iran, wondering what they spent all those hours doing. Did they crouch on the floor in moldy cells, scratching out Morse-code messages to each other? Did they get bread and water through a rusty slot in the wall? Even hostages, I figured, had to have something to keep them busy.

I tried to interest Rew in the subject, but he only frowned and shook his head. He'd settled into his own kind of routine, spending part of each day staring out his bedroom window at the drive or ticking off the days it would take for someone to come.

"What about that man who tried to sell us a vacuum that time?" he asked me.

"He hasn't been back since Gran said we prosecute trespassers," I said.

Rew sighed. "Well, Adele Parks might show up."

"If she's not on vacation yet," I said, getting uneasy.

He gritted his teeth. "It doesn't matter. The police will catch him. Just wait until they see that letter."

The thought satisfied him for a full day, but by the end of the first week, he'd taken to parking himself on the stairs and glaring at Andrew Snow, as if he could will the entire Sunshine police force up the road, guns drawn.

"What's taking so long?" he asked me the afternoon of the eighth day. "They should be here by now."

I could hear the desperation in his voice, and my stomach went liquidy, but I just shrugged, trying to find excuses.

"Maybe the mail's slow," I said. "Or maybe they thought it was a joke and ignored it."

"They wouldn't do that," he said with heat in his voice. "They'll come."

And all the time, that letter sat hidden in my dresser upstairs, where I'd stuffed it after coming home. It made me sick to think of.

If things had been different, I might have sought out Gran, to see if she was in a talking mood. But Gran came down now only at night, and she never spoke.

Sometimes she'd give me a little smile or brush my cheek with her hand when she passed. It was good to feel her there. But she'd never stay if I tried to say anything, and if Andrew Snow started up, she'd put her hands over her ears and rock or just turn and walk upstairs as if she hadn't heard a thing.

Of all of us, the one who'd settled into the clearest pattern was Andrew Snow. Besides trying to talk to Gran and sitting quiet in his chair by the door, he'd begun to take an interest in our kitchen. Reading in the paper that only a handful of men had been caught seemed to give him energy, and after that first investigation of our cabinets, he'd turned the whole room into a project. He cleared the old cans and empty jars from the counter, lugging them down to the cellar in a big bag. Then he found the pots we'd buried under old papers and garbage in the broom closet.

With nothing better to do, I watched him at it. Besides, though he had threatened us and though he held us in the house, I was interested in Andrew Snow. I couldn't help but be.

He wasn't much like Rew really. True, he had the red hair and the light skin. And those big, round eyes so like my brother's. But he had barely any freckles, and his eyes were brown, like mine.

After a few days with us, he'd found clothes for

himself in a pile Gran had kept in the closet, or maybe in the large paper bags down in our smelly basement. When he came up, clean, in them for the first time, I was startled at how much he looked like a regular man; like anyone.

Sometimes after that, I'd try to imagine him in one of the stories I'd told Rew. Once or twice I could almost do it, but then Andrew Snow would look my way or Rew would shout at him, and it would disappear. And I would think how I hated Andrew Snow, the angry man.

Still, after a while, I found a few things I liked about him, even though I didn't exactly want to. For one, I liked the way he talked.

When he was done threatening us and just talked of regular things — like what we'd have for supper — Andrew Snow's voice had a steadiness to it. It didn't sound like a voice that kept secrets. So I wasn't so surprised when on day eight, Andrew Snow told a story. It was about my mother.

"You look like her" was how he began it. He'd been watching me flip through one of our old magazines, plenty of which could be found under our couch. I was peering at pictures of Fairfield County, where, according to *Life*, smart New Yorkers had their summer homes.

I looked up, startled. "Like who?" I asked.

"Like your mother," he said. "Just like her. I should

have realized it when I saw you first, but I never knew her that young."

This statement fascinated me, and I put aside the certain knowledge that Rew would brand me a traitor for engaging in communication with the enemy.

"I do?" I said. "Wasn't she pretty?"

He gave me a strange look. "She was," he said. "Very pretty. That's the first thing everyone said about her."

All of a sudden, my head started buzzing again. I tried, but failed, to fix on the image of a pretty woman with brown hair like mine. Despite my better judgment, and knowing as I said it that I was breaking Gran's rules, I asked:

"What was her name?"

It was his turn to look startled.

"You don't know her name?" he asked.

I shook my head.

"It was Amanda," he said. "Amanda White. We used to joke about the fact that she switched her name from White to Snow."

I sat very still, letting this news settle. My mother's name was Amanda. She was pretty. She laughed at jokes.

From nowhere, a hot wave of anger washed through me. "She didn't," I said.

Andrew Snow looked puzzled. "Didn't what?" he asked me.

And I was confused again. Didn't women who laughed at jokes leave their babies? Is that what I thought? I knew they did. They probably laughed lots of times. But it wasn't a nice-sounding laugh, like he made it seem. It was an ugly laugh. Too loud. Unmannerly, as Gran would say.

Andrew Snow was watching me. I glared at him. "She left us, you know. She said we were all your idea."

Something changed in Andrew Snow's face then. His lips pressed together and made a hard little line, and he blinked his eyes fast, those round eyes that were too like Rew's.

"She was high-spirited," he said. "Funny and smart, but young. Too young, maybe, to have responsibilities. It's true, I was the one who wanted kids." He seemed about to say something else but stopped there. I looked at him, waiting. Angry as I was, I wanted to hear more about Amanda White, who was young and funny and didn't want me.

But Andrew Snow stopped talking then. Stories about my family always seem to be short. I looked down into my lap and noticed I was crushing the picture of one of those pretty summer homes in Fairfield County.

Chapter 21

Andrew Snow started in on Gran again that night. He marched upstairs, rattled her doorknob, and started talking.

"You can't stay in there forever," he said. "You're going to have to answer me sometime."

I came up behind him. "You don't know Gran," I said. "She'll stay in there for as long as she wants. Just leave her alone. Can't you?"

He looked at me, a sorry kind of a look, but then he rapped sharply on Gran's door. "Just tell me the reason," he said. "I just need to know the reason. Didn't you think I'd ever come home? Is that it?"

Rew had been in his room across the hall with his door closed. He came out when he heard Andrew Snow.

"You've made her crazy," he said in a strange, frozen voice. "She hates you. She wasn't ever this bad before."

Andrew Snow said nothing. But later, he found me in the kitchen, where I was trying to wipe off a sticky part of the counter so I could make myself a sandwich with the last of the bread and some chunky peanut butter.

"We're going to need another supply run soon," he said, looking into the cabinets. It made me queasy to think of, with that letter waiting upstairs. But I didn't say anything.

For a minute, I thought he was wondering why I didn't, but then he bit his lip and asked me a question I didn't expect.

"Your gran," he said. "What's she like? Usually?"

I liked the word he used, so I said, "She's better than this, *usually.*"

He seemed to think he needed to explain something to me as he looked round the kitchen. "I didn't know this was how you lived," he said. "I knew you were with her, but—I didn't know she'd gotten this way after my dad died."

It took me aback to think of him having a dad. And, for that matter, of Gran having a husband. She never spoke of him, but then, most of her stories about herself stopped when she was ten years old, and other than that, she talked about no one but the people in *Life* magazine, and me and Rew.

"She's not this bad always," I said again, feeling the need to defend her. "Lots of times — mostly — Gran is just a little bit funny. But she cooks for us and stuff, and we're not hungry."

Usually, I said to myself. Besides, when she went into her bad times, I was big enough to shop and cook.

But Andrew Snow was looking round the kitchen again. "In prison," he said — so matter-of-factly he might have said "at work" or "at the grocery store" — "I work in the kitchen."

"What do you mean?" I asked him.

"I mean that's my job," he said. And he sounded almost like he might laugh. "Over there. You didn't think we sat around in tiny cells all day, did you?"

Actually, that's exactly what I had thought, but I decided not to say it. I just looked at him. I was thinking that I'd always wondered what job he had. And all the time I'd imagined him flying planes or making secret treaties, he was just past the Zebra Forest, working in the kitchen.

It made me wonder for a second if my mother, Amanda White, was out somewhere walking around this very minute. Maybe in a store, shopping, or at the movies, carrying that brown purse of hers. The thought made me grit my teeth.

"It's a good thing to keep kitchens clean and in order," Andrew Snow was saying. "I learned that. It makes things easier. And you don't get sick as often."

"We don't get sick," I protested.

"Well, that's good," he said.

Andrew Snow was full of surprises. When he wasn't threatening us, he was worried we might get sick eating off dirty plates.

"You could always clean it, if you care that much," I said.

And Andrew Snow surprised me again. "I guess I will," he said. And he found a towel and got started.

If I had been Rew, the minute our father turned his back to scrub the sink, maybe I'd have knocked him on the head with the nearest frying pan. But there was something nice about watching him work there, as if he planned to make us a meal and worried that we ate in an unhygienic environment, like Adele Parks did. And actually, once Rew did wake up, into the second hour of that four-hour cleanup, he didn't run anywhere. He just stood in the kitchen doorway next to me, watching. Andrew Snow noticed him, too, but he didn't say anything. He just kept on working.

Chapter 22

After that, I found that Andrew Snow knew quite a lot about hygiene. This is possibly something they teach you in prison. I don't know. But he certainly spent a lot of time improving the hygiene of that kitchen.

"I'm surprised you haven't gotten sick before now," he said when he found a stack of dirty dishes festering under the kitchen sink. "You're growing enough mold here to make penicillin."

Since I had never heard him make a joke, I started to defend Gran, but he stopped me.

"She was always a great cook, you know," he said. "When I was a kid, she made a lot of pancakes. Every morning almost."

This was one thing I had figured out myself.

"She makes them for us sometimes," I said.

"My father liked pancakes," he said. "He could eat stacks of them in the morning. He said farmers have always known breakfast was the most important meal of the day, and they'd eat pancakes even before dawn."

"Was he a farmer?" I asked.

Andrew Snow did laugh then. It was a strange, happy sound. A minute after he did it, I couldn't figure out how that laugh had come out of his face. But then, I'd seen Rew laugh a billion times, before Andrew Snow came. It was kind of like that.

"No," Andrew Snow said. "He lived all his life in the city. But he loved the country. The woods, especially. He had all these nature books, and he'd read them at night, learning about trees and wildlife and such. He said that one day he'd retire out here, probably to a place just like this one. He never did, though."

"Why not?"

Andrew Snow didn't answer for a little bit. He stared out the kitchen window at the Zebra Forest. "He got sick," he said finally. "He didn't have time."

I looked out at it, too. Until Andrew Snow came, I hadn't been away from the Zebra for this long ever, not even in the coldest winter. I tried to imagine my grandfather, always wanting to come out to the country and never getting to.

116

"I don't remember him," I said after a while. "He died when I was little."

Andrew Snow nodded. "That must have been when she moved out here," he said.

"Gran, you mean?"

He nodded again. "She wrote me. She said she couldn't stay in that old apartment of theirs without him. Especially not with me — away. But she didn't say where she would go."

I couldn't think what to say to that. But Andrew Snow didn't need me to say anything. He just stared out at the Zebra, quiet. At last he said, "They loved each other with a passion, those two."

I stood there looking out at the Zebra, too, wondering where Gran, who kept every magazine she'd ever subscribed to, had put all the pictures of her husband, my grandfather, the man she'd loved with a passion.

Chapter 23

The next morning, I went on another supply run. This time, I didn't mind the bus ride, didn't worry that people would know. But when I passed the blue mailbox, I felt that familiar drop in my stomach.

Before I'd gone downstairs, I'd taken the letter and stuffed it back in my pocket. I knew by now I was never putting it in the mail. But I couldn't seem to figure out what to do with it. Then I noticed a garbage can, one of those public ones that sit on the edge of playgrounds. There was a little park near the bus stop, and I could put the letter in there just as easily as I could put it in the mailbox.

I crossed the street to get to it and stood over it for a minute. When the sidewalk emptied, I pulled out Rew's envelope and looked at it again. It had gotten crumpled from sitting in my dresser and pocket so long. But the red EMERGENCY still stood out bold as anything.

I dropped it in the garbage can, my heart pounding, and turned to go. Then I thought what would happen if the garbage man saw it and opened it. No. That wouldn't work. So I went back and plucked it out.

My hands were sweating, and they left smudges on the envelope. I couldn't keep carrying it around. What if it dropped out of my pocket? What if Rew found it? A man passed me on the street, and I shoved the letter back into my pocket, then took it out again. Rew had written that EMERGENCY big enough that someone could see it from across the street, I thought. I tore open the envelope.

Then I started ripping. I just tore it all—the envelope and the letter—into tiny pieces. No one could read it when I'd finished with it. And I let the pieces fall, like snow, into the garbage can.

All the time I was doing it, I could see Rew, sitting there writing that letter on his bed. See him happy. And my chest ached, and my eyes smarted. My hands were even shaking. But I couldn't send that letter. I knew I never could.

It took me a long time to pull myself together after that. I went and sat on one of the swings in the little playground, sat there holding tight to the chain, letting my feet push me back and forth gently, till my heart stopped rattling my ribs so hard. And all the time I kept thinking that if Rew knew what I'd done, he would never, ever forgive me.

Chapter 24

When I made the bell ding at the Sunshine Grocery I found Molly back at her TV watching, and it was a relief to find something that felt normal.

Andrew Snow's list this time included not just vegetables but a bunch of cleaning supplies, some of which I'd never heard of. He'd made me take a knapsack, even, so I wouldn't have to carry it all in my hands. That's how much he wanted me to buy. I knew Molly would notice and thought about what I might say to distract her when I got to the counter.

But Molly, cracking her gum with a vengeance, wasn't one to let things go.

"Looks like someone's making a project of it" is what she said when I set a bottle of bleach, scouring pads, and Windex on the counter. Plus a bottle of vinegar, which

Andrew Snow said is a great natural cleaner. "It's a little late for spring cleaning, don't you think?"

I wasn't sure if she was joking, so I tried to think of a reason for her. "Well, we've got time now, in the summer," I said. "I guess that's why."

Molly sighed. She pushed her hair back off her face and then shook it out behind her. "Lots of people having time on their hands in this town," she said. "I don't suppose you've heard, but there was a major layoff at Enderfield. A bunch of guys are out of work."

I didn't know what she wanted me to say to that, so I asked, "Did they catch the people? The ones that ran away?"

Molly shook her head, and the brown wings in her hair did a little jump. "Just a few. And now the FBI had to come down and take photos from the prison files to put up at all the post offices. The warden's in the doghouse, if you know what I mean. My boyfriend's brother-in-law works in the office there, and he said it's likely the warden will be out any day."

Molly blew a huge bubble and popped it loudly. I could smell the fruit flavoring from across the counter.

My heart started beating a little faster, and I took a breath, trying to slow it. "What happens to the people they catch?" I asked. "The prisoners?"

She shrugged. "Do I know? I guess if they try to

fight, they get it, don't they? They're fugitives, after all —
and dangerous, I'm betting, too. Now the FBI's on their
case, they'll be looking all over the country. They'll get
them back. You don't go messing with the FBI. Those
guys are professionals."

I noticed suddenly that Molly kept the air on too
high in the Sunshine Grocery. It was giving me a chill.
"Oh," I said. "Yeah."

Molly cracked her gum then. She was just getting
started. "The question is, What's going to happen here in
town in the meanwhile? It's a shame, is all I can say. All
those people out of work."

"Will they bring them back?" I asked her. "The ones
they catch? To Enderfield?"

She tilted her head, considering, while she chewed.
"Probably. I mean, there's not unlimited space round the
country, you know? Unless they do something real bad
while they're gone. Then I guess they'd ship them off to
maximum security."

I didn't know what that was, but it sounded bad.

Molly went on, "But my boyfriend's brother-in-law
says that if the warden has a word to say about it, they'll
all be right back here. He calls them his 'population,' and
he plans to fight for them."

"I thought you said he's going to lose his job," I said.

"Yeah, well, that's likely." She laughed. "But then, the

one that deserves it is usually the last canned, know what I mean?"

I didn't, but she went on: "He's making announcements, that warden is. All about security changes. And maybe it'll save him. Who knows? The top dog's always the last to fall — that's what it seems like from my side of the counter." And she laughed again.

I didn't care much about the warden, but Molly's line of conversation was making me jumpy. I glanced at her TV, hoping to find something to distract her. Phil Donahue wasn't on, but there was a news program going. Pictures of the Ayatollah Khomeini, a furious-looking old man with a beard and turban, flashed on the screen behind her. I nodded toward it.

"He's the head of Iran, right?" I asked her.

She looked, cracked her gum again, and nodded. "Oh, yeah. Crazy maniac. But they let one out, you know. Yesterday or today, I think."

"A hostage?" I asked her, surprised. "How come?"

"He was sick," she told me. "So they let him go home."

I paid for my things then, and Molly helped me put them in the bag. The bottles were heavy, and I arranged them carefully in the knapsack before I slung it onto my back.

Molly nodded her approval. "Good thinking," she said. "Save your back."

I heard her snap her gum one last time before the bell dinged as I let myself out.

All the way home, I thought about hostages let free just for being sick. I wondered if Andrew Snow knew that even Iranian mullahs did that. But then I thought about the FBI, and what they might do to fugitives. They were experts, after all. Probably sharpshooters and everything. They probably didn't even have to come inside to kill you. They could get you right through a window.

Of course, they had to know you were there first.

Chapter 25

On day thirteen, Adele Parks came to visit. I saw her from the front window, parking her car at the end of the road that turns to gravel when it hits our property. Adele Parks didn't like to drive up all the way because of the time her car got stuck in the mud that collects along our unpaved drive. She had to pay a tow truck to pull her out, and ever since then, she's parked down at the end and walked up.

When Andrew Snow saw me looking, he jumped up and backed away from the window, fast.

"Who's that?" he wanted to know.

"That's Adele Parks, a lady who visits us once in a while," I said. "To see if we're okay. She's not coming here for you."

"Who talks to her, usually?"

"I do."

"And your brother?"

"Sometimes," I said. "Not always. Not a lot."

Before Rew could do anything, Andrew Snow grabbed him round the shoulders and put a hand over his mouth.

"Go talk to her, then," he said, handing me the key and nodding toward the kitchen door. "Outside."

I looked from Andrew Snow to Rew, whose eyes were more outraged than afraid. I think we knew by then that Andrew Snow wasn't going to hurt anybody.

"What're you going to do to him?" I asked.

"Nothing," he said. "But he'll yell if I let him go. You just go talk to her till she goes away."

I knew Rew would have told if he were me. Maybe if she'd come a few days earlier, I would have. But not anymore.

I went outside to meet her.

"Hello, Annie," she said. "How's summer treating you?"

I smiled nice and wide.

"Wonderful," I said. "It's great. You know I like vacation."

"Anything fun doing? Reading anything? Did you get any summer work to do?"

I shrugged. "I don't remember. Probably not. But I'm reading lots, you know. I just read *Robinson Crusoe*. That was interesting." That was a lie. I'd read *Robinson Crusoe* the year before.

"There's a summer reading program at the library in town," she said. "Maybe you'll come out to it."

"Maybe," I said.

"Your grandmother around?"

"She's sleeping."

"And Rew?"

"Out back," I said, jerking my head in the direction of the forest. "Building a tree house."

In books I've read, kids always build tree houses. This is considered a good way to spend your time, and I thought Adele Parks would approve. She did.

"That's good," she said. "You tell your grandmother I stopped by, won't you?"

I nodded. "I'll walk you to your car," I said.

Adele Parks and I had an unwritten pact. She knew Gran wasn't maybe the fittest parent figure around, but she'd once told me, when I'd gotten a bit too elaborate in my lies to protect her, that she wasn't going to take us away from her anyway.

"You can trust me, Annie," she'd said then. "I'm not going to separate you from your grandmother. That wouldn't be good for anyone. Just promise me that if anything was *really* wrong, you'd tell me."

I'd always thought that was a decent promise to make, and one I could keep. But it turned out to be like a lot of my other promises: impossible. So I broke our pact and walked her back to the car, smiling and lying all the time.

Chapter 26

When I got back to the house, Andrew Snow was relieved, but Rew was furious. He couldn't think of enough names to call me, and when he ran out of them, he rushed upstairs to his room and slammed the door.

I went upstairs to try and talk to him. If he'd have thought about it, he'd probably have locked me out, but Rew was too mad to think just then. I peeked into his room. He was lying on the bed, staring red-eyed at the ceiling.

"Don't hate me," I said. "Adele Parks isn't the right one to tell. She'd just think about Gran and how bad she's doing, don't you see?"

Rew rolled over to look at me. "That's not why you didn't tell," he said. "You don't want them to take him away — that's why."

Then he sat up, and he looked at me hard, thinking. I got scared then. I should have left the room, but I wasn't fast enough.

"Where's the letter?" he asked me.

I tried to say I'd sent it. I wanted to blame it on the post office, but I was tired of lying to Rew. I hated it. So I didn't answer him.

He looked at me, and I saw his face going red and white as his eyes widened.

"You said you sent it," he whispered.

I looked away from him then. But he knew.

"I hate you, Annie," he said, and he wasn't shouting it, but he meant it — I could tell. "I *hate* you! Get out of my room. Go be with Andrew Snow if you love him so much."

Rew turned his back on me then, just as he had with Andrew Snow. I stood there, blinking. Crying wouldn't help me, I knew that. He wouldn't care one bit if I cried now. Maybe he wouldn't have cared right then if I'd jumped out the window. He might even have been happy.

I looked down at the floor, anywhere to take my eyes off Rew's back. And there, beside his bed, I caught sight of *Treasure Island*. I leaned down to pick it up. The book fell apart in my hand. He'd torn it into three pieces.

I took it with me when I went downstairs. Now I

really didn't have anyone to talk to but Andrew Snow. I came down carrying that broken book, my throat so tight I could barely breathe, and sat down at the kitchen table.

Andrew Snow was busy at the stove when I came in. He glanced over at me. "You two okay?" he asked.

I stared at him. Did he think Rew had forgiven me just because he couldn't hear the yelling downstairs? Did he think it was no big deal, what I'd just done?

Okay. The word made my blood boil.

"No," I said, my voice low. "No, we're not *okay.*"

He turned to look at me then, holding the spoon so it would drip over the pot of soup he was making.

"Annie," he said. "Give him a little time. He'll get over it."

He talked like he knew Rew. Like a real father would. But he didn't know anything about him. Not about either of us. I wanted to throw something at him, but all I had was Rew's broken book.

"What do *you* know?" I said. "You don't know anything about it! You don't know the first thing about Rew. Or don't you remember that you haven't ever been around here before?"

He frowned. "That's not what I meant," he said.

Once I'd gotten started, I couldn't seem to stop. I practically spat the words back at him. "You do a lot of things you don't mean," I said. "Like coming here. You didn't mean that, either, but you did it, and you ruined everything! She was okay before you came! She was good!"

He flinched at that, and I could see his hand tighten on the spoon.

"Good?" he said, his voice low. He waved a hand to indicate the kitchen. "This was good?"

I glared at him. "It was *okay*," I said. "And you came and messed it all up. That's what you *do*, isn't it? Mess things up? Is that what you did when I was little? Is that why my mother ran away?"

I saw the spoon drop into the pot, and in the same instant he was moving toward me, his face suddenly white. I flinched, pulling *Treasure Island* up to shield myself. But he didn't hit me. He just stood there, an inch or so away, chest heaving, towering over me.

Slowly, I looked up into his face. He was standing there, lips pressed together, staring down at me. And the expression on his face confused me, because as I watched the color creep back into his cheeks, he looked more hurt than angry.

I pushed my chair back cautiously, and a piece of *Treasure Island* fell onto the floor between us. He looked down at it, then leaned over and picked it up.

For what seemed like a long time, he stared at the

broken piece in his hand. Then he said, "I think I can fix it, if you want me to."

I wasn't sure I could get my voice to work just then, so I shrugged, but after a second, I laid the other pieces on the table. He picked them up gingerly.

"All it needs is some good tape," he said. "There's some downstairs. But you're missing the front piece."

When I finally got the words out, they were no louder than a whisper. "That was never there," I said. "Those are the pieces we always had."

Andrew Snow didn't say anything. But he went downstairs, got the tape, and put Rew's book back together. While he was doing it, I sat at the table, watching the soup boil in the pot.

Chapter 27

All afternoon, silence stopped up the air in the house. Rew hadn't talked much in general since Andrew Snow came, but it was different knowing he *wouldn't* talk to me, even if I wanted. By evening, I was ready to scream, just to hear the noise. Instead, I sat down with Andrew Snow for supper.

The soup he'd made was filled with all the rest of the vegetables in the bin. I'd never seen such lumpy soup.

"Why'd you put this in?" I asked him, making a pale, round ball duck and bob in my bowl.

"It's a turnip," he said. "They're good in soup. Sweet."

I watched Andrew Snow eat. I noticed he ate all the soupy part first and saved the vegetables for the end.

"We don't usually get turnips," I said.

"I don't wonder," he said. "Mom always hated them. She didn't like any root vegetables much. I remember she once said she didn't like eating things that grew with their heads in the dirt. We had a lot of tomatoes, though. My father used to come home, close his eyes, and guess what was for dinner before he came in the kitchen. If he was stumped, he'd say to me, 'Well, at least I know we're having tomatoes!'"

I smiled at that. I'd never known my grandpa was a funny man. Maybe that's why Rew loved jokes so much.

"Your father," I said when he got up to get me a second bowl. "What did he do?"

"He owned a shoe store," he said. "A little one, in the city."

"But he wanted to be a farmer?"

Andrew Snow smiled at that. "Maybe," he said. "Or a woodsman. Who knows? He certainly loved the country. He took me to the mountains once, when I was nine or ten. Taught me how to find my way in the woods by the direction of the sun, and about the plants there, that sort of thing."

"Like what?" I asked.

Andrew Snow stirred his soup. "Well," he said, thinking, "like, there are kinds of mosses that can get totally dried out — they can look dead, even — and then they perk right up with the first rain. He loved that sort of thing. He loved knowledge in general. A big reader, my father."

"He must have hated the shoe store, then," I said.

Andrew Snow shook his head. "Oh, no, not at all. He liked people, too. Always reading and learning things and talking to the customers. He knew everything about feet, for example, and shoes. You know there are legends about shoes? He used to tell one about the emperor Vespasian, back in Rome. He said that Vespasian was a general laying siege to the Holy Land, and an old wise man came to talk to him there. While they were talking, Vespasian started putting on his shoes. He got one on, and a herald came in to tell him that back in Rome, the emperor had died, and he was to be the new one. After that, Vespasian couldn't get on that second shoe. He didn't know why until the sage told him that good news makes your feet swell. That's the kind of thing my father loved. Stories like that."

I studied Andrew Snow, eating his vegetables across the table. He hadn't shaved since he'd come to us, and a light red stubble had come out on his face, the hint of a beard that would be almost the color of his hair. Behind him, through the window, the Zebra Forest was collecting shadows as it edged toward twilight. It was Gran's favorite time out there, and I tried to picture her upstairs. Maybe she was watching it now, like she used to. On good summer nights, Gran liked to come out and sit on the old glider behind the house, a prize she'd hauled over from someone's front yard in town, where they'd put it out for junk.

She'd sit there, rocking and picking at the rust on the seat, watching the darkness soften the edges of the Zebra. That's what she called it—softening. It was a word I liked. Now I thought of her, upstairs, silent. She was different than I'd imagined, almost as different as the real Andrew Snow. She was a woman whose husband loved people, who sold shoes and talked and read, and who loved trees. She was a woman who made pancakes and loved tomatoes and had a son who went to the woods and learned about moss that could live, even without water.

Andrew Snow was watching me. I saw that when I looked his way again, from the window. He didn't turn away, and I felt awkward a moment. So I asked, "What did you want to be, before? A woodsman, like your dad?"

He cocked his head at that, as if trying to remember. "I did like the trees," he said. "Liked them a lot. But I liked books even better. You'll laugh when I tell you what I had planned."

I shook my head. "I won't," I said.

He smiled then. Andrew Snow's smile made me forget a lot. And I forgot enough to smile back at him. "I wanted to be a librarian," he said. "I thought they read all day."

Chapter 28

Once I knew he loved books, I found the best of them for Andrew Snow. I figured as long as he spent half his time by the door, he might as well have something to read. And he did read, but he also sat by the door less. He spent a lot of time in the kitchen, keeping it in order and getting our meals. And one day he even started on the front room as I watched him from the stairs.

On day fifteen, Rew came back down from his room. He didn't say anything to me, and certainly not to Andrew Snow, but he settled himself on the couch and pulled out his chessboard and pieces.

"Want to play?" I asked him. He ignored me, and I saw he was setting the board to play Fox and Hounds. Fox and Hounds is how Gran started teaching us to play chess. Instead of using all the pieces, you just use four pawns and one bishop. The fox has to try and get to the other side of the board, moving diagonally only on the black pieces, and the hounds have to try to stop him from doing it. If the hounds surround the fox, he's captured, but if the fox gets through to the other side, he wins. You'd think the hounds would have the advantage, since there are more of them, but it isn't true, because each of the hounds can move only one space at a time, and they can only go forward. So if you're hounds, and you move one of them forward and then realize you've left a wide-open space for the fox, too bad for you. Rew loved being the fox, because he always found a way past me, no matter how deliberately I moved those hounds. Just like in real chess, I could never beat him.

I hated the game, because I hated pawns in general. When we played chess, my pawns got knocked off right and left, and I considered them pretty useless. Gran told me that pawns were an important part of the game. True chess masters, she said, knew how to use their pawns. I wondered if Rew was in that category.

We hadn't played Fox and Hounds in a long time, but I was so lonely for Rew, I'd have played anything. "Can I be the fox?" I asked him.

"You're not playing," he said. "I'm playing myself."

"What?" I said. "That's like playing tic-tac-toe against yourself. It won't work. You always know the other side's next move. You'll stalemate."

He didn't answer that, just moved his fox out onto the first square.

Andrew Snow came out of the kitchen to watch.

"He won't stalemate," he told me. "The fox will win. At least at first."

Rew snorted at that. "What would you know about it?" he said. "You don't even know how to play."

"Your gran taught me, a long time ago," Andrew Snow said. Rew didn't look at him, but I could see he meant to try to win with the pawns, just to show Andrew Snow.

He took a long time with it, but he couldn't cheat, moving the pawns back when he made a mistake. We were watching. So the fox broke through.

He blew a bubble of air out in frustration, making his bangs jump. But he put the pieces back and tried again. The fox won that time, too.

"You'll only win with the pawns if you learn how to make them move forward without breaking the line. You can't open a space, or the fox wins," Andrew Snow said.

"I'm not stupid," Rew answered angrily. "I know that. And who asked you to watch, anyway?"

He gathered up his pieces and moved to the stairs then, settling himself on the landing at the bottom with his back to us. But even there, I could see him setting up the pieces again and again. Rew was nothing if not stubborn.

Chapter 29

Andrew Snow had been at our house for more than two weeks when he began thinking long-term. I could see this because he started stocking our cabinets. On day eighteen, he sent me out not just for the regular groceries but for a few things I'd never heard of—like wheat germ.

"It's good to have a supply of staples," he said, explaining that he didn't mean the kind that stuck paper together, but things that kept well in the kitchen. "Things you can add to dishes, or make soup out of, or use when you're running low on groceries."

Wheat germ didn't appeal much to Rew.

"I thought germs were bad for you," he said suspiciously when I showed him the list. "Sounds more like poison than food."

"I think this is a different kind of germ," I said. "Besides, I don't think they sell poison at the grocery store."

Rew looked like he wasn't too sure. But I didn't care, because at least he was talking to me again. He spent a lot of time with his chessboard, but he was back on the couch with it, and when I said something to him, he answered.

I was so worried about the strange things on the list that I took the bus an extra stop, all the way to the big grocery store on the other side of town. It was the place I'd lost Rew in, and I hated it, but at least Molly wouldn't be asking questions about who thought to tell me about wheat germ.

The Super Mart was ice-cold inside and smelled like a hospital. Even the floors looked glossy, and I wondered what in the world someone was wasting all that shine on, when all it reflected was feet. But they had wheat germ, and everything else, and no one said a word to me there as I pushed my cart up and down the aisles.

At the checkout, I picked up the local newspaper, which was always on Andrew Snow's list. On the front page, a big headline announced that the warden had been cleared of all responsibility for the riot and would keep his job, which showed that Molly knew what she was talking about. In the lower right-hand corner, they even had a story about the newly released hostage, who was in Switzerland, getting tested for something called "neurological problems." I didn't know what kind of problems those were, but they sounded serious. And the government was saying people shouldn't get their hopes up that any other hostages would be out anytime soon. I figured that meant you had to be nearly dead before they let you go, over there in Iran.

I didn't see anything more about Enderfield or about how many prisoners had been brought back. But I folded the paper in half and put it carefully in with the groceries. And then I bought some gum. I thought I might try cracking some on the way home.

When I brought the groceries in, Rew came to the kitchen to watch me unload the wheat germ, along with everything else. It had been almost more than I could carry.

Andrew Snow looked with satisfaction at his staples, which included flour and sugar and cornmeal — things that made other things, instead of just canned goods and bread, which was more what I was used to buying.

"Wheat germ is good for muffins," he told us, starting to pour ingredients into a big bowl. "It adds a lot of vitamins, and you don't taste it a bit."

He sprinkled some of the light-brown flakes into his muffin batter.

"I'm not eating those" was all Rew said.

He did, though, once I'd eaten one. And he stayed in the kitchen that afternoon, watching Andrew Snow bake. He wouldn't say a word, but he didn't leave, either.

This didn't mean he had given up on his war with Andrew Snow. Later, I found Rew sitting in the front room, alone, staring at the door.

"He thinks I won't go tell anymore, but I will," he said angrily. "I'm just not doing it yet. I don't want to upset Gran."

I didn't point out that Gran, who had not spoken for days, seemed pretty well past being more upset. Instead I said, "You should talk to him, you know. You wouldn't believe it, but he can tell stories."

"I don't want to hear his old *stories*," Rew said. "I don't want to hear anything from someone who *kills* people."

Rew was right, I knew. He had always been smarter than me, and he was now. But the problem was, I couldn't see the angry man so much in Andrew Snow. I looked for him, plenty. I looked for him when Andrew Snow made muffins, or read books in the chair by the door, or told about his father, who taught him about moss in the woods. I looked for him, trying to put the pieces of

Andrew Snow together. But no matter how hard I tried, I just couldn't do it.

And so for a while, I pretended, like I'd always done out in the Zebra Forest. Only this time, Andrew Snow wasn't a test pilot or a spy. He was a librarian. My father. And he was on vacation with us for a while, because it was summer and his library had closed.

Only Andrew Snow wasn't very good at pretending. On day nineteen, he stood by the kitchen door, peering through its little square windows at the Zebra.

"I used to look at those trees all the time," he said when he heard me come into the kitchen. "But I never saw all of them. The wall blocked them. I never realized how nice the trunks were, too."

I looked out the back window to the side of the door, realizing with a start that he had washed it. I could see the Zebra Forest clearly, those white trunks and deep brown ones bright in the midday sun.

I tried to pretend he hadn't mentioned the wall.

"The white ones peel," I said to him. "The bark comes off in strips, and we write on them sometimes, Rew and me. We have a whole pile of bark messages buried out there."

Andrew Snow nodded at that, but he didn't stop looking at the forest. "I used to spend a lot of my free time looking at the tops of the trees," he said. "Back in prison. I liked the fall, especially. The leaves turn orange and red then, and I liked to think how much my father would have loved this place."

I sighed. The word *prison* didn't fit in with my library pretending, so I gave it up.

"Is that why you came this way?" I asked him.

He didn't answer for a while. He left the window and went to the sink, washed his hands, and took out the vegetables, getting ready to start dinner. He was quiet so long, I thought he wouldn't answer me. I thought maybe I'd stumbled onto one of his rules, found a question that silenced him. But after a while, when he was sitting at the kitchen table, he said, "I guess that's it. I hadn't really thought of it. A few weeks before the riot, some of the guys were talking about running. I didn't pay that much attention. I didn't think they'd ever do it. They all liked to talk, especially during meals. And they said if they ever got a chance to run, they'd head down the highway, get a car somewhere, and head straight for the city."

"How come?" I asked.

He shrugged as if the answer were obvious. "You could lose yourself easier in a city, I guess."

Lose yourself. I'd never heard anyone say that before. I didn't like the idea of it at all. But I thought I might know what it meant.

"So that's what they did?" I asked.

"I guess so. Once they'd gotten the gates open, that's where they all ran to. Half the prison ran out down the highway. But I just turned around and went round the back, to the woods. No one else did. The guys had all said you'd lose your way in those woods and probably starve. But I didn't think so. I'd been in woods once or twice. Besides, I wanted to see what those trees looked like up close. Maybe that was it."

Until he said it, I hadn't realized that I'd been hoping something. Sometimes you don't know you want something until you don't get it. But when Andrew Snow said that, I realized I'd been wishing he'd been lying that night when he acted like he didn't know we were there. I'd been hoping he had come looking for us. It was only when he told me about the trees that I knew it wasn't true.

Chapter 30

By the end of July, when Andrew Snow had been with us almost three weeks, the first of the summer thunderstorms came rolling in. The windows darkened, and the sky turned yellow, the way it does when the last of the sun squeezes its way past the gathering clouds. I was looking at it out the front windows when the rain started. It hit the windows like a handful of pebbles.

"Summer storm," I said to Andrew Snow, who'd been straightening Gran's magazines. "We get a lot of those. Especially when it's hot like this."

Then I felt stupid, because I realized that he'd been right on the other side of the Zebra all along. He knew about our summer storms. He didn't say so, though.

"Electricity builds up in the air," he said instead. "It's got to go somewhere."

Rew came down then. He sat on the steps and stared out the front window. Rew and I loved storms, because Gran loved them. We looked at each other, but neither of us said anything.

It wasn't dark yet when we heard Gran's door open. I thought she was just going to the bathroom, then back to bed, but then Rew said, "Annie," soft, like a warning.

I looked up and there was Gran, at the top of the stairs. She was wearing a robe and slippers, and her hair went every which way, but she smiled a little when she saw us, and started coming down.

Andrew Snow was in his place by the door, reading one of the books I'd given him. He looked up when Gran came down, but I blocked him, standing so Gran couldn't see his face.

She smiled at me again, and her eyes weren't dull, the way they'd been so often lately. She went on into the kitchen. I followed her.

Behind me, I heard Rew whisper to Andrew Snow.

"Don't ask her questions," he said. "Don't bother her."

Gran was moving toward the cupboard, looking for the mugs. Andrew Snow had moved everything, of course, in his cleanup. I wondered if Gran would notice.

"Can I make you some hot cocoa, Gran?" I asked her. "It's raining."

Gran nodded. "I would love that, Annie B.," she said.

It was one of the first things she'd said in weeks, and I grinned. But behind her, Andrew Snow came in.

"I'll do it," he said.

For a minute, I froze, wondering what Gran would do, if she would run back upstairs and go away from us again. But after a minute, she gave a little half smile and nodded. So I sat down next to her, at the table, and she took my hand.

It's hard to know with Gran, I thought. *Hard to know what makes her happy and what makes her sad.*

Gran watched Andrew Snow make the hot cocoa, and I watched Gran. So did Rew, who had come just inside the kitchen. When the good smell of the cocoa filled the room, Andrew Snow set a cup down in front of Gran. Then, without asking, he set down three more.

I liked the look of those four cups. I sneaked a glance at Rew, in the doorway, but he just shook his head. He turned and went upstairs, and from the kitchen, I heard his door snap shut.

Neither Gran nor Andrew Snow seemed to notice. Andrew Snow cleared his throat and sat down.

Gran took a sip of her cocoa and smiled that faint smile. "It's good, Andrew," she said. She still held my hand.

"Thanks," he answered. Then he reached over and touched her hand, the one that held mine, on the table.

"And I want to say thank you too for keeping . . . for all this time, for Annie and Rew."

Gran didn't answer. She squeezed my hand, and didn't let go to take his, and after a minute he pulled his hand back, and put it in his lap.

I shifted a little in my seat. "We don't have to talk," I said to Andrew Snow, hoping he'd take the hint. "Let Gran drink her cocoa."

For a little while, we just sat there, listening to the clatter of rain on the windows and to the boom of the occasional thunderbolt. The windows would light up around us, and Gran would give my hand an extra squeeze. All the time, she watched Andrew Snow, but Andrew Snow didn't look at anyone.

Finally, Gran said, "They're both smart, Andrew. And good. Always good."

I thought Gran might be getting ready to tell one of her excellent lies, but Andrew Snow looked up at her, quick, and I could see by the way he narrowed his eyes that he just couldn't help himself. He was going to have his say.

"Couldn't you have let me know?" he asked her. "I'm still alive back there, Mom. We didn't both die."

The color that had been starting to show in Gran's face drained away. She turned from him and stared at the gray window, at the storm.

"No one's coming this afternoon," she said. "No one would go out in such a storm. That's good."

I didn't have any idea what she meant, but Andrew Snow seemed to. And it made him angrier. He stood up.

"Is that what you think?" he asked her. "Is that what worries you? Why would they come? Why would they? How would they even know?"

Gran let go of my hand. She put her hand to her ear again.

"Don't!" I said to Andrew Snow, my voice rising. "Don't talk to her!"

He stopped then, but it took a lot for him to do it. I could see his jaw jut out on either side, he was holding his mouth so tight. And the grim look had come back to his face. With an effort, he sat back down.

It was too late. Gran stood up, so fast the chair fell back behind her. I couldn't tell what her expression meant, whether she was frightened or sad. Before I could puzzle it out, she was at the landing, and then I heard her door swing shut upstairs.

Andrew Snow had not moved from his chair. I felt like Rew just then. I wanted to tell Andrew Snow how much I hated him. How much I wished he would just go away. Instead, I said something almost as mean.

"How come Gran never visited you?" I asked him,

trying to make my voice as cold as Rew's. "Can't you get visitors in prison?"

I could tell I'd hurt him, because he looked down at his hands when I said it, as though his knuckles were the most interesting thing in the world. He tilted his head, in the way I'd seen Rew do so many times, when Adele Parks came and asked him questions he didn't like answering, like whether he had many friends.

But he answered me anyway, and he didn't sound angry, either.

"She came once," he said, and I guess he saw that I didn't believe him, because he added, "It was years ago, right at the start. She came with my dad. He was alive then. But it killed the two of them, coming there. Her especially. She just touched the glass and didn't say a word. And then, after he died — she didn't come any-more. I think maybe it was just too hard."

If I'd thought hurting Andrew Snow would do me good, I was wrong. I could picture him too well, sitting there in that prison, with nothing to look at but the trees. But I knew Gran. And I knew she'd never go to a place like that. Not for anyone. Not even for her son.

Chapter 31

Everyone had gone silent. Gran, Rew, Andrew Snow. For a full day after Gran went back upstairs, Andrew Snow barely said a word, and Rew didn't come down, either. But I was sick to death of silence, sick to death of slamming doors and people who ran and hid. So on day twenty-two, I decided I wasn't going to be afraid of them anymore. Not Gran, not Rew, and not Andrew Snow.

That morning, my father made oatmeal with wheat germ sprinkled into it.

He spooned it out for me. When I didn't reach for it, he said, "Eat. It's good, really."

I ignored that, both him and the oatmeal. Instead, I said, "Why are you so mad at Gran? What did she ever do to you?"

Andrew Snow looked at me in surprise. "I'm not mad at her," he said. "I'm grateful she's taken care of you all this time."

I snorted, sounding like Rew. "You're a liar," I said. And I didn't care if it hurt him. "Every time you talk to her, you end up yelling."

Andrew Snow sighed. He turned from me, took a rag, and started on the kitchen window, where pink still lingered in the sky over the Zebra. I could smell the Windex on it, a sharp, chemical smell. I thought he meant to ignore me, but he didn't. After a while, he said, "That's true. I'm angry and grateful at the same time, I guess. I can't decide which. Don't you ever feel two ways about something?"

I almost laughed. I felt two ways about almost everything. But he didn't mean for me to answer. He moved on with his rag, cleaning the stove.

"So?" I asked him. "Are you going to tell me?"

"Annie," he said, turning round to look at me. "Haven't you wondered why no one's come for me? It's been almost a month. No one's come to find me."

I hadn't expected him to say that. "You said they'd look for the others first," I said. "Isn't that the reason?"

"For a while," he said. "For a while. But I should have been gone by now. I've overstayed my time. By now, they're hunting for anyone they haven't found by going to their families, the people they know. Don't you see that?"

I did.

"So why haven't they come?" I asked him.

He sighed, in that way Rew does when I'm being slow.

"Because as far as anyone knows, I have no family. My family's gone," he said to me.

If Rew had been there, he would have understood. I felt dull, blank.

"But we're here," I said.

Andrew Snow sat down. It was as if all the air had gone out of him suddenly.

"For two months after I went to prison, my father came to visit me," he said quietly. "Then one day, he didn't wake up. Just died, in his sleep, there in the apartment. Your gran sent word to the prison, but I wasn't allowed out for the funeral, and she didn't come see me. And then, just a few months later, she sent a note."

"A note? You mean like a letter?"

"No, just a note. Twenty words, no more. It said, 'I can't, Andrew. Forgive me. I have to be free of this place. And the children should be free too.'"

"Free? What did she mean?"

"She meant she was leaving. I didn't believe it at first. Leaving me there, with no one. But she did it. She picked the two of you up and she disappeared. Totally."

"How do you know? You couldn't have come out anyway."

"I sent my lawyer. He was a nice man, did his best for me. He went and talked to her friends, went looking. She'd done a good job of it. She didn't want to be found. She closed every bank account they had, paid all her bills, left no forwarding address. Sold anything that could have led anyone to her. He looked for a long time, my lawyer. But he couldn't find a trace of her. Not of any of you. The only one he did find was Amanda."

I gave a little start. "Amanda? My mother?"

He nodded. "*She* wasn't hiding, anyway. He found her and went to talk to her. He asked if she'd help him find you, so I'd have someone on the outside, someone just to write to, even. So I could know about my kids as they grew up."

"What did she say?"

Andrew Snow ran his fingers through his hair, and it stood up, dark red. Then he closed his eyes and took a long breath.

"She said you weren't her problem anymore, and neither was I. She called the prison and told the warden I had people harassing her. I spent a week in isolation for that."

I felt sick. The smell of the Windex and the aroma of the oatmeal seemed to clog my throat. I pushed the bowl away, to the edge of the table. Andrew Snow opened his eyes.

"I shouldn't have told you that," he said softly. "I'm sorry. Some things, maybe, you shouldn't know."

But that only made me angry. I wanted to know things. I wanted to know everything. Even things about Amanda White.

"Why did she hate us?" I asked him. "Were we so bad, then?"

Andrew Snow blinked. He shook his head. "You weren't bad," he said softly. "You were babies. Just babies. It wasn't you. It was her. Something was broken in her. I see it now. After she had you, she got a little hard, somehow. She went rushing around after good times—that's what she always called them. She was always looking for something to do—night and day. Most of the time, she left you with your gran, and after a while, you even stopped crying for her when she did. There was something missing in her, I guess. I don't know what it was, what made it. But she could laugh—she could always laugh. And yet I never did see her cry. Not once."

I thought about that. About a mother named Amanda who was broken. And I thought about Gran.

"Is Gran broken, too?" I asked him.

He put his chin in his hand then, thinking. But finally, he said, "Gran left everything she knew behind.

After what happened with me, she couldn't even look her friends in the face anymore. Shame does that to a person."

He stopped then and looked down at the table, smoothing the grain of the wood there with his hand.

"I did that to her, I guess. That was my fault."

Then he looked up again, and straight at me. His eyes were bright. "Shame can change a person, sometimes," he said. "It changed her. But I don't believe it broke her, Annie. No. She's hurt, but she's not broken. Not like Amanda was. Gran left me, maybe because she couldn't help me anymore. But she took you with her. Didn't she?"

Chapter 32

Rew had grown almost as still as Gran. He no longer played Fox and Hounds or read, and he didn't ask me questions, either. He lived in his room and on the stairs, and he hadn't eaten at the table since the night of the first thunderstorm.

I missed him terribly. So on day twenty-four of our captivity, I decided to try something I hadn't done since he was small. I took *Treasure Island* out from my closet, where I'd hidden it after Andrew Snow had put it back together, and let myself into Rew's room.

Before Rew had started school, he'd been what Gran called a terror, maybe because he was bored then, before he could read. He'd have tantrums—fits of temper so bad he'd rip the front room to shreds, and Gran would have to pick him up and just hold him tight while he struggled and screamed and sometimes even tried to bite her. I was all of six or seven then, and I'd just watch her while she held on to Rew for dear life, scared he'd hurt her with all that flailing and screaming. And one day he'd gotten a hand loose while she held him, and he threw it back and caught her right in the face. She wasn't hurt, I don't think, but she was stunned, and she let him go. She sort of gave up after that, and Rew went pulling books off shelves and throwing pillows off the couch until he just tired himself out.

Gran told me then just to let him alone. He'd just have to work through it, she said. She couldn't stop him. But I couldn't stand all that screaming and mess. So after a while, I got to thinking about bribing Rew, offering him something so he'd calm down. I tried candy and pennies and promising to read to him an extra book at night, but he was so angry, he couldn't even hear it.

Till one day I stopped trying to talk to him, and just took a book and opened it, right there on the sofa, while he raged all round me, and in a quiet, regular voice, I just started reading. I just sat there pretending he wasn't screaming and throwing things. I read the way I usually did, turning the pictures around to show him, just as if he'd been sitting calm as anything on the floor in front of me. I didn't shout over him, didn't try to get him to hear, but he could see my lips moving, I guess, could see me turning the book to show the pictures, and it must have gotten the better of him, because after a while, he stopped for a second, to hear what I was saying. And then he hushed his crying so he could listen. After a while, he sat down next to me, tantrum forgotten, and let me finish the book. Soon I could get those tantrums to stop nearly as soon as they started, and he'd even help me clean up, just so he could get the next story.

Rew wasn't screaming anymore, but he was mad. So mad he couldn't think straight. And so now I settled down on the floor of his room and opened up *Treasure Island,* to one of my favorite parts, the chapter when Ben Gunn scares the pirates as they make their way toward the treasure, with Jim Hawkins as a captive. He sings pirate songs in the woods and then calls out Captain Flint's last words, "Darby McGraw! Fetch aft the rum, Darby!"

I decided to start right in the middle, from the best part.

"'The buccaneers remained rooted to the ground, their eyes starting from their heads,'" I read, keeping my voice low. "Long after the voice had died away they still stared in silence, dreadfully, before them.

'That fixes it!' gasped one. 'Let's go.'

'They was his last words,' moaned Morgan, 'his last words above board.'

Dick had his Bible out, and was pray-
ing volubly. He had been well brought up, had
Dick, before he came to sea and fell among bad
companions."

I paused, sneaking a quick look at Rew on the bed.
He lay there, his back to me, not moving. But he wasn't
asleep. I could tell that by how fast he was breathing. So
I started again.

"Still, Silver was unconquered. I could hear
his teeth rattle in his head, but he had not yet
surrendered.

'Nobody in this here island ever heard of
Darby' he muttered; 'not one but us that's here.'
And then, making a great effort, 'Shipmates,'
he cried, 'I'm here to get that stuff, and I'll not
be beat by man nor devil. I never was feared of
Flint in his life, and, by the powers, I'll face him
dead. There's seven hundred thousand pound
not a quarter of a mile from here. When did
ever a gentleman o' fortune show his stern to
that much dollars, for a boozy old seaman with a
blue mug — and him dead, too?'"

Usually, Rew couldn't get enough of that part. Long
John Silver's scared to death, but he'll fight a ghost, even,
for that treasure. Of course, it's Ben Gunn all along, and
after a while, the pirates get to recognizing the voice. But

they don't know Gunn's alive, so they think it's his ghost that's singing. And they never thought much of him, I guess, because they're not even afraid of his spirit. I took up the story again.

"'Why, nobody minds Ben Gunn,' cried Merry; 'dead or alive, nobody minds him!'

It was extraordinary how their spirits had returned, and how the natural color had revived in their faces. Soon they were chatting together, with intervals of listening; and not long after, hearing no further sound, they shouldered the tools and set forth again, Merry walking first with Silver's compass to keep them on the right line with Skeleton Island. He had said the truth: dead or alive, nobody minded Ben Gunn."

I looked up again at Rew, but he still hadn't moved. This was the part we liked best, where we'd laugh because all the time it's Gunn who's got the treasure. The joke is on those pirates.

But Rew wasn't laughing.

Still, my old trick worked, because as I went on, voice steady, just reading, Rew rolled over. Except he was still mad.

"You could have told Adele Parks," he hissed at me. "You *should* have."

I shook my head. "I couldn't, Rew. Don't you see it would have been just the same?"

He frowned, getting up on one elbow. "What, you think she'd have hurt him? She'd have known how to do it!"

I didn't know how to explain it to him. And Rew was glaring at me so hard I knew he'd probably never listen, but I couldn't help myself. I wanted to make him see.

"It would have been the same in the end. You know it would! She'd have called the police!"

He sat up and stared at me. "You think they're never going to find him, don't you? You think he can stay here always."

"No, I—"

But he didn't let me finish. "They're going to get him sometime," he said, the heat in his voice rising. "And they'll put him back where he belongs. It's going to happen. The only question is how."

I shook my head, but he pressed on.

"She'd have known how to do it," he said firmly. "You could have made her promise."

It hurt me to say it, but I had to. "Nobody keeps a promise like that," I said quietly.

"You should know!" he spat.

I didn't know what to say to that. I looked down at

the book, thinking to change the topic, but he wouldn't let me. He moved to the edge of the bed and leaned down toward me.

"He's a *murderer*, Annie. He *killed* a man. Don't you ever think of that?" he asked me. "Don't you ever?"

I did. I thought of it a lot, but I couldn't explain that to Rew. "Maybe he's sorry," I said weakly. "Maybe he's changed."

Rew laughed, and not in a nice way.

"Sure," Rew said. "Sure. That's why he ran out here and took us prisoner. He's so *nice* now. He's not bad at all."

"Gran knows what he did," I said. "And she doesn't seem scared of him."

Rew looked at me like that was too stupid a thing to even answer.

"You know he's bad, Annie," he told me, and his voice got stronger as he talked. "You're just lying to yourself, thinking he isn't. But you'll see. You wait. You'll see how bad he is."

I didn't know what Rew meant, and so I left him, taking *Treasure Island* with me. But I couldn't stop thinking about what he'd said. Maybe Andrew Snow was exactly like Long John Silver, nice one minute, rotten the next. Maybe he was sly like that. Maybe I *was* lying to myself.

But it didn't *feel* like a lie. Then again, it didn't feel

like Andrew Snow, the son of that smart shoe-store owner, could have killed a man.

On day twenty-six, almost a month after Andrew Snow had come, I finally decided to ask him.

The house had been quiet all day, and hot. Gran didn't love the air-conditioning too much, and we rarely turned it on. But Rew and I usually spent so much time outside, we barely noticed. We did now, stuck in the house with the doors closed. Upstairs, we'd opened the windows, and a breeze rippled in from the Zebra, but downstairs, we were stifling. Andrew Snow, making spaghetti and some kind of sauce at the stove, dripped with sweat. I came in to find him wiping his red face with a dish towel. He looked out at the sky over the Zebra. Clouds gathered there.

"Another storm," he said. "It'll be a big one, too, given the heat."

Then he did something that made my heart thump. He took the key out of his pocket and opened the kitchen door. Cool air blew in, and it brought the Zebra with it — the smell of leaves and bark and grassy places.

"We need air in here," he said, by way of explanation. "There'll be a lot of good wind before the storm."

Rew was upstairs; so was Gran. I thought if Rew felt the breeze whip up the steps, he'd be down in a minute, running free. But maybe not.

I took a deep breath, and maybe the open door helped me ask him. "Andrew Snow?" I said. "Why did you go to prison? Did you really do what Gran said?"

My father stood very still. Then he dropped his head down to his chest, lifted his hand, and rubbed the back of his neck. I could hear the rusty old glider creaking in the wind and the leaves rustling in the Zebra. After a while, Andrew Snow closed the door and sat down at the kitchen table. I stood there, quiet. I could tell, knowing him a little now, that he wasn't ignoring me. He was thinking.

At last he said, "Yes. I did."

I didn't say anything.

"It was manslaughter. Do you know what that is?"

I shook my head.

"It's when you do something that you didn't plan to do."

I waited.

"I mean . . ." Andrew Snow struggled for words. The steadiness was gone from his voice. "It's when you're angry, and you don't think what you're doing, and you just — you do something you regret later."

I looked at him a long time, wondering. Wondering if you could be the angry man once but not always.

He spoke after a while. "Back then, I did things without thinking sometimes. Especially when I got mad.

170

When I was younger, I never really thought before I did things. And when someone pushed me — I guess I just let myself go. I never stopped to consider whether I had a choice about doing something, even if I was angry."

I watched him, but he didn't seem like he meant to say any more.

"What were you angry about?" I asked him finally.

He looked at me, then past me, out at the Zebra again. "A lot of things, I guess. I can't excuse it, really. Back then, I got mad often. And I was mad that night."

I didn't move, I was listening so hard.

Andrew Snow sighed. It was a tired, sad sound, like the air going out of him, and he looked pale and worn down. He caught my eye for a minute and then looked away, down at his hands.

"Your mother hated the sound of a fussy baby. I mean, nobody likes it, but for her, it was like fingernails on a blackboard. If you can believe it, I was supposedly the steady one back then."

He frowned and shook his head. I waited.

"I tried to show her when you were small how to bounce you and calm you down, but she didn't even want to try. She said the sound grated so much. She wasn't a person to be patient with that kind of thing. So we made a kind of system. I told her to just give it five minutes. You could stand anything for five minutes, right? And then if she couldn't stop you crying, I'd take you. It got to be kind of a private joke with us. You could stand anything for five minutes, right? Only it turned out—" He sighed, pressing his lips together as if to stop himself from continuing. I watched him, thinking about Amanda White, trying to picture me, small and red and crying, and how they'd try to rock me. I couldn't see it. But then Andrew Snow went on, and all I could do was listen.

"That night — well, I could hear the sound of a baby crying all the way down the street when I came home from work. We lived on the third floor — that's how loud it was." His voice seemed to drop as he talked.

"Things hadn't been good for a while. She told me she was leaving, told me more than once, but I always managed to get her to change her mind. My mother took the two of you so she could go out. Give her a break. So when I heard the crying, I ran up to the apartment, thinking I'd take him. The baby."

Rew, I thought.

"But Amanda wasn't there. Your gran had you. Said Amanda had gone out somewhere. It didn't take me long to find her. There was this bar she liked. They had dancing. I found her there with a stranger. They were the only two dancing, she and this thin guy with dark hair. He was holding her. I could tell they'd been drinking when I got over to her. He was whispering something to her and she was laughing when she saw me. She didn't even step away. Just turned her back and kept dancing."

He was staring at his hands so long I think he'd forgotten I was there, but finally he started again. "I pulled him off her. That's when she got mad. Told me to give it up. To go home and stay there. She asked me, hadn't she given me enough? Hadn't I gotten what I wanted?

"No, I said. No. I wanted her."

He glanced up at me then and jumped a little, as if he'd forgotten I was there, listening. He started to fidget; he got up and went to the sink but didn't turn the water on. He just stood there, looking out the window. After a while, he started up again.

"Amanda laughed when I said that, about wanting her. If you would have known her — known how she could be — well, you'd know why it made me happy to hear her laugh. I thought for a second she'd come home, like she had before. But then he started laughing, too.

"He asked her how she could have possibly fallen for a guy like me. And I saw her smile and thought we were okay. But she said, 'Oh, I did. Sure I did. For about five minutes.'"

Andrew Snow seemed to be struggling for breath. His chest heaved, and he stopped for a minute, maybe to get some air. But then he said, "That guy, he looked my way, laughing harder than ever. Then he said, 'Well, you can stand anything for five minutes, right?'

"He was still laughing when I grabbed him."

Andrew Snow shuddered.

"He fought back at first, but I was bigger, and stronger, and much madder. I just threw him down. I heard his head hit the floor. Such a hard sound, like a piece of wood, almost. I should have stopped. Amanda was screaming, pulling at me, but I was so mad, I kept picking him up and shoving him back. Three times, four. He had such dark hair, I didn't even see the blood until it seeped out onto the floor."

I looked at Andrew Snow's back. He was taking big gulps of air, breathing hard. I thought he was done, but then, quieter, he said, "If I'd have pushed him just the once, they'd have called it an accident. But I kept doing it. I kept picking him up and shoving him down. That's manslaughter. That's what they said. And it is. I didn't plan it, Annie. But I killed him. I killed him just the same."

Chapter 33

When he finished talking, Andrew Snow leaned over the sink and put his head in his hands. He started to shiver a little, like I'd seen Gran do. I left him there, shivering a little myself, and went to sit in the darkness of the front room. It wasn't hot anymore. Already I could hear thunder grumbling over the Zebra, and I wished I could find one of Gran's quilts and throw it over my head to shut it out. I didn't like the noise now, and the dark, what with Andrew Snow shivering in the kitchen and Gran and Rew buried upstairs in their rooms.

But Rew wasn't upstairs. I sat down on the couch, kicking away *Life* magazines, and noticed him there, sitting on the bottom step of the stairs.

Even in the falling dark, his face was white. I jumped a little when I saw him, round eyes so big, staring at me.

"Rew," I said. "Sit with me. It's going to storm."

Rew didn't answer. But he turned his head to look out the front window, at the first arrow of light slicing down into the edge of the Zebra. He said not a word as the sky opened up.

The rain came in a great gust, slamming into the windows. The light was all gone now, and neither of us moved to turn a lamp on. Lightning frosted the windows every few minutes, making them blink against the hammering rain.

Upstairs, I heard a door open. Gran, dressed in her robe, drifted downstairs, peering out at the storm. Rew didn't move when she stopped just past him, at the window over the stairs. Andrew Snow came out of the kitchen then. He looked at me, then at Rew, and Gran.

Gran put her hand flat on the windowpane, and I saw it turn black against a sudden surge of light. She turned away from it and reached down to touch Rew's head.

I thought she must have given him a shock, because he jerked away when she did that. I'd never seen him move that quick before.

"Don't touch me!" he screamed at her. And the sound of his voice made even Gran's eyes go wide. Rew backed away as if she'd hurt him — fast, into the middle of the room. His face was ghost-like against the dark of the front room as he looked from Gran to me to Andrew Snow.

"Rew—" I started, but he didn't let me finish. He was shouting, shouting in a voice so high I thought it must belong to someone else. Someone I didn't know.

"No!" he shrieked. "You stop! You stop! You *want* him here, Annie, you do, but I don't! Don't you think I know you're letting him stay? He even told you—he told you what he did! And you're not going to send him back! Not you, and not Gran!"

And then he turned on her, and he did something I'd never seen him do before. He grabbed Gran's arm and yanked it from the window. "Why did you bring us here?" he screamed at her before I could move to stop him. "Why? Why? You never went to see him anyway!"

I didn't understand him for a moment, with all that screaming, and with the knocking of the rain and the thunder smashing over our heads. But when I looked up at Gran, I could see that she did. She was looking across the room at Andrew Snow, and when I turned, I could see that he understood, too.

Gran lifted up her hand, out toward Rew. But Rew, enraged, batted it away. "No!" he screamed. And in a fit, he ran to the front door, pulling against it, rattling the chain there. He couldn't get it open.

Everyone else seemed frozen. Andrew Snow stood watching him, and so did Gran, her hand still half up. But Rew moved in a frenzy. He yanked and yanked at the door, screaming in frustration. And then his head came up, and he turned, and in a second he had run for the kitchen, past Andrew Snow. I felt a sudden gust of wet wind and knew he had opened the back door.

"Rew!"

Gran screamed it, behind me. Her voice was shaky and high against the sudden noise of the storm, but I heard her. Barefoot, in her robe, she moved fast, too, into the kitchen, out into the night.

I ran after her, to the doorway, and felt the rain on my face. Andrew Snow had followed them, sprinting into the darkness. A clap of thunder boomed overhead, then the Zebra flashed into view and I could see the three of them silhouetted against it, running in the rain.

For a moment, I stood there, trembling. Then I ran, too, out into the rain, toward the Zebra.

Chapter 34

Like great white bones, the birches stood out in the darkness. I ran toward them, calling, screaming for Gran and Rew and Andrew Snow. But the rain, coming down in sheets now, washed my voice away, and the wind roaring down through the Zebra took my breath, too.

I reached the edge of the woods and slipped into mud, falling on a root. My face slammed down into the moss, and I could smell the wet, the green water everywhere. But I got to my feet and ran forward, into the Zebra. My heart beat so hard I had to gasp for air, but I knew they were in there somewhere — they couldn't have gone far.

The rain swept over me, slapping my face, soaking my clothes. But if I was cold, I didn't feel it. All I knew for a while was running, the sensation of wet ground, and the crashing thunder and the sharp pain of twigs tearing at my arms in the dark. Panting, I followed the jagged path of white trees that glimmered there, straining to hear voices over the thrashing of wet leaves overhead, the branches whipping back and forth in the wind.

Deeper into the Zebra, the dark thickened. It clung to the trees, clotted there between the trunks, and made even the white birches vanish. After a while, I could only stumble forward, hands reaching out, calling, calling.

But soon I was lost. I'd never been lost in the Zebra before, but then, I'd never been in such darkness. I looked behind me, but I couldn't see even the edge of the forest. I couldn't see home.

If I'd thought I'd been frightened when Rew ran into the night, I found out then that fear could hollow you out so fast, it left you weightless, erased. Standing there in the wet, roaring darkness, blind and lost, a terror so fierce took hold of me, I nearly fell down. Water dripped off my face and down my fingers, and I reached for the nearest tree and clung to its rough bark, arms tight round it, to keep myself standing. I blinked, trying to clear my eyes of water, but the night was so heavy, all I could see was black.

Thunder exploded over my head then, setting my ears ringing. At the same moment, the forest flashed into sight. If I hadn't been holding the tree, I'd have fallen to the ground, and as it was, the trunk, even the roots, shook. A sharp hiss and the smell of burning came then, and I shut my eyes, dazzled by the afterglow of the flash.

Another crash, and again I saw the forest, electrified. This time I forced my eyes open and strained for a sight of the edge. When the third strike came, I saw it. Letting go of the tree, I ran for home.

No one had come back. I stood shivering, blinking in the too-bright kitchen, letting the water spill off me into a puddle on the floor. After a while, I realized I was sobbing, and I breathed and stopped myself. I went upstairs and stripped off my clothes, changed, and pulled a quilt off my bed, wrapping it round me to stop myself from shaking. Then I went downstairs to the kitchen, to wait.

I could see now, staring at the windows, why Gran hated them so at night. No matter how hard I strained my eyes, I could see nothing outside. Just my own ghostly face reflecting back at me, alone, in the empty kitchen.

After a time, I couldn't stand it anymore, and I closed my eyes, putting my head down on the kitchen table.

I didn't sleep, though. In the early hours of the morning, when the storm had died down some, I heard the kitchen door and lifted my head.

It was Rew. His hair and clothes were slicked and brown with mud, and his skin stood out against it, washed unnaturally clean by the blowing rain. He stood for a moment, blinking in the doorway, and then he stepped back and held the door open. Behind him came Andrew Snow, looking much the same as the first night I saw him, dirty and grim. He was carrying Gran.

Chapter 35

Get towels," Andrew Snow said. "Quickly."

Without a word, I turned and ran upstairs. Rew followed. We carried down armloads of old bath towels. I tried to hand one to Rew, so drenched he was dripping, but he barely noticed me.

Andrew Snow had laid Gran on the couch in the front room. He had a dish towel in his hand, and he was gently wiping blood from her face.

I stopped short when I saw that. Gran's eyes were shut tight, and a long, ugly gash ran from her forehead to her cheek. Andrew Snow turned and saw us, reached for the towels, and quickly wrapped Gran in them, rubbing her body to warm her.

Beneath the towels, he pulled away her wet things.

"Get me something, a robe or nightgown," he said.

I brought him down her old flannel nightdress. From her bed, Rew had brought her big quilt, and Andrew Snow threw it over her, pulling on her nightdress under it and pulling the quilt tight around her, like a cocoon.

When he'd done that, he turned and looked at Rew.

"You get warm, too," he said, "or you'll be sick."

Mute, Rew turned and went upstairs. Andrew Snow pulled a chair over to the couch and sat down, leaning over Gran. He gently touched the edges of the cut on her face and pressed his palm to her cheek.

"Lightning struck one of the trees out there," he said to me. "I think a branch knocked her coming down."

"Will she be okay?" I whispered.

"I don't know," he said. "I think so. The cut doesn't look too bad, but she lay there for a while. Rew found her before I did. When the storm died a little, I heard him calling. And I found them."

Gran moaned then, though she didn't open her eyes. Andrew Snow put his hand on her head again, and she subsided.

"We should make soup," Andrew Snow said. "She could use something warm when she wakes up."

But he didn't move. He kept looking down at Gran, his hand on her head. So I said, "I think I could make some."

I thought I knew how by that time, having seen my father do it so often.

In the kitchen, I opened the cabinet and found the staples Andrew Snow had said would come in handy. Tomato sauce, dried peas, rice. I cut up carrots and added some spice and poured it all into the big pot, to heat on the stove with some water. I even sprinkled in some wheat germ.

I went out to tell him I was making her tomato-and-rice soup and found that Rew had come back down. He was clean and dressed in dry things, but he wasn't sitting back on the stairs. He'd drawn a chair up to the couch, where he was watching Gran's silent face, not two feet from Andrew Snow.

I stood looking at them from the kitchen door, and I realized that with all that had happened, there was just one thing I really wanted to know. I wondered, when he found Rew there beside Gran, who Rew had been calling.

Chapter 36

Gran opened her eyes just after dawn. The storm had gone, and outside, the rising sun caught in the lingering drops and sent sparks of light into the front room. Rew had fallen asleep in his chair, his head thrown back like a rag doll, but Andrew Snow still sat by Gran, unmoving.

I hadn't slept, either, but had settled myself in a nest of towels and quilts on the floor, watching Andrew Snow watch Gran. So I saw when she stirred, groaning softly, and opened her eyes. She looked fuzzily up at Andrew Snow, sitting quiet there, and he gave her a little smile.

"You're okay," he said.

Gran's eyes seemed to focus, and I thought she might try to sit up and run, remembering all that had happened. But instead she smiled back, a little, faint smile.

"Andrew," she said, and her voice was her own again. And then all of a sudden her eyes filled, and her lip trembled. Her voice dropped to a whisper, so I had to strain to hear it. "I didn't mean to take it all away," she said. And then she added something I couldn't hear.

Andrew Snow put his forehead down into his hand and rested it there for a while. Gran never took her eyes off him. Finally, he lifted his head, and I could see wet around his eyes. But he smiled at her again, anyway.

"Maybe it was better," he said quietly. "That they got to grow a little without knowing—" But he didn't finish what he was going to say. Instead, he looked out the window, at the edge of the Zebra. "Dad would have liked this place," he said. "Lots of sunshine and trees."

Gran smiled when he said that. A real smile, like before. And Andrew Snow put his hand gently on the quilt and patted her shoulder. He stayed that way for a long time, until she closed her eyes and dropped back to sleep.

After a while, Andrew Snow moved from the chair. The first thing he did was lift Rew and carry him upstairs. Then he came down and went to the kitchen, and soon I smelled pancakes cooking.

The smell must have woken Gran, because she opened her eyes, turned, and saw me there, on the floor. I got up, untangling myself from the quilts, and went to her, taking Andrew Snow's place.

"Gran?" I asked.

"Hmm?"

"It's me, Annie."

"I know it is, beauty. I got hit on the head. Didn't get my brains knocked out."

I decided not to mention the phantom she'd become those past few weeks.

"Gran?"

"Yes?"

"You know Andrew Snow?"

Gran turned to look at me full in the face then, wincing a little as she did it. The cut on her head was dry now, but it must have hurt.

I couldn't read her expression, but she said, "I know him."

I wanted to ask her a lot of things. And tell her a few, too. But some stories are too well worn to be retold. Some lies have to be let be. And besides, I had missed Gran. So I didn't start in with all that again. Instead, I said, "He makes good soup."

And she smiled and said, "Yes, he always did."

And then she went back to sleep.

Chapter 37

The house grew quiet again after that. Not just because the rain had stopped hammering the windows and the wind had fallen away, either. The silence came from all of us now. But it wasn't a bad silence, like before the storm. It was like the Zebra sometimes at midday, when the birds are just tired. Gran was no longer a phantom, but she was worn out. She lay on the couch and let Andrew Snow sit with her and bring her soup and find her the books she began, once again, to read.

As for Andrew Snow, he was in the kitchen or by Gran or sometimes just standing, looking out the back windows at the Zebra.

Then there was Rew. If Gran had come back to us, Rew had gone further away. He walked around without a word, and if I looked at him, he'd look somewhere else. He didn't sit by me or Gran but perched again on the stairs, hands between his knees, for hours. I saw him watching Andrew Snow.

Another thing. We both went out back again. Our father didn't tell us we could, but on the second day after the storm, Rew walked past him in the kitchen, opened the door, and went out. Andrew Snow didn't say a word.

We didn't go to the Zebra Forest, but after that, we went out behind the house, just to sit and look at it.

A few days after the storm, when Gran got up from the couch on her own for the first time and swayed and had to sit down again, Rew went out back and sat for a long time. Finally, I went to him. After the storm, I'd lost count of my days, and I'd forgotten how long the hostages had been in that embassy in Iran. But I knew that my father had been with us for more than a month.

It wasn't much time, not enough for me to even grow half an inch, I thought, but when it came to Rew, it struck me that he looked different. Something in his face had set.

"What're you thinking about?" I asked him, sitting down beside him on the rusty glider. He didn't look at me when I asked him but swung his legs and kicked at the chipping paint of the glider, and squinted into his knees.

"Nothing," he said.

"I'm getting tired of 'nothing,'" I said. "I've heard 'nothing' for half a week now. You want to be like Gran? Is that it?"

He shrugged, still looking away from me.

"I'm not like Gran," he said, his voice husky. "I'm what she said all along. I'm like him."

He dipped his head in the direction of the kitchen.

"Like Andrew Snow?" I said, taken aback. "Like him?"

Rew nodded. He looked down into his palms and swallowed, as if to keep the words back. But at last he said, "I hurt Gran, didn't I?"

"You didn't!" I protested.

"I did," he answered back, fast this time. "I opened the door. I was angry, and I ran out, though I know better. I forgot. That's how mad I was."

"You didn't hurt her," I said again. "The branch did. The lightning."

"Yes," Rew said, and he was himself again, that reasonable, thoughtful kid who always won at chess. "But I opened the door. I knew better."

"Not then," I said.

"No," he agreed. "Not right then."

He was quiet once more, thinking, and I didn't interrupt him. It struck me that Rew might be like Andrew

Snow, but at least he wasn't anything like our mother. He didn't run away from things.

"One thing's different," he said after a while.

"What's that?"

"You don't go to jail for opening doors," he said.

I didn't have an answer for that.

After a long time, Rew got to his feet. He walked out into the yard and kept walking, all the way to the edge of the Zebra Forest, to the first blanched tree. He leaned against it, looking out into the shadows. I didn't follow him. After a while, he came back toward the house. When we turned to go in together, we saw our father, watching from the back window.

Chapter 38

Two days later, Andrew Snow announced that he was going back. Gran wasn't there. He'd told her earlier and she'd disappeared upstairs, behind a barricade of magazines, to think about it, maybe, or to forget it. But he was waiting for us at the table for breakfast late in the morning, and he'd put on his washed prisoner's uniform and looked pressed and ready to go.

Rew looked at him but didn't say a word.

"Why?" I asked. "Why not Mexico? Or Canada?"

He shrugged. "I'm done running away," he said. "If I go back, I'll be done eventually."

"But you didn't mean to do it!" I protested. "You said so yourself! You've been there long enough!"

My father shook his head, but he didn't answer. He looked away from us for a time. Finally, he said, "I didn't mean to, but the fact is, I did do it. And I'll pay for it. And then I'll come back."

He had a hard time looking at us. He studied the grain of the table and spaces in the kitchen he'd cleaned.

"Five years is a long time," he said. "Will you . . . will you keep up here?"

I thought he must mean the kitchen. And the rest of the house. "I'll try," I said. "Gran likes to hold on to things, you know, but I'll try."

"I'd like to hear about it," he said. "If you decide to visit."

This hadn't occurred to me. I looked at Rew, who was also studying the table grain. He made no move to answer. "I'll visit," I said. "I promise."

"I'd like that," he said. Then he stood. He shook my hand. Rew didn't look at him, and he stood there a moment longer, waiting. Then he went to the door. At the last minute, Rew looked up.

"Thank you for carrying her back," he said quietly. "Gran."

Our father nodded. He looked at us both a minute longer, and then he sighed, opened the door, and was gone. We didn't move from the table. We didn't rush to the window to see him walk out across the yard, past the rusty glider, to the Zebra Forest. I don't know what Rew was thinking, but I knew that I didn't want to see him disappear between the trees.

Still, after a while we got up. We cleared the breakfast dishes. We washed them. We put them away. And Rew even swept the floor.

Chapter 39

When school began again, we both went. And I found that it wasn't so bad to get up and go each morning. Beth came back from camp, and we had a good English teacher, Miss Penn, who seemed interesting. I wasn't ready to tell anyone about my summer just yet. So when Miss Penn asked for the traditional end-of-summer essay, I wrote instead about my grandfather, the shoe-store owner who knew all about Vespasian.

I brought that essay home to Gran, and she read it on the couch, leaning over it, with her eyes close to the words. When she was done, she looked up at the stairs like she might run to them. I felt my shoulders pinch tight as I wondered what she'd do. But then she smiled at me, even though her eyes looked like they might cry.

"This is a good story, Annie B.," she said. "Your grandfather was such a good, good man." I let her keep my paper, and later I saw her put it in the drawer by her bed. Then we had lunch together and played cards.

Rew began reading *Treasure Island* again, and once I knew he wasn't going to rip it, I let him have it back, to keep in his room. He still liked Long John Silver lots, but he got interested in other characters, too, ones he'd never paid attention to, like Captain Smollett.

"The squire Trelawney's just an idiot," he said to me one afternoon in the Zebra. "He talks too much, and he hasn't got sense enough to keep even a treasure map secret. But the captain — he smells a rat from the first. Plus he knows how to run a ship."

I continued to make my case for the doctor, but I conceded the point. It was good, anyway, to get back to talking pirate slang. "Yup," I said. "That squire, what does the captain tell him?"

Rew grabbed the book and flipped to the place. "'Treasure is ticklish work,'" he read. "'I don't like treasure voyages on any account, and I don't like them, above all, when they are secret, and when (begging your pardon, Mr. Trelawney) the secret has been told to the parrot.'"

I laughed out loud at that. "Blabbed, he means!"

"And by the squire!" Rew shouted. "See? An idiot!"

That fall, on Sundays, I started going round to see my father. Gran wouldn't go. She couldn't. But she let me talk about Andrew Snow. Sometimes she'd even ask about him. And after I told her, she didn't go upstairs, but she'd give me a smile and say, "You want to hear the story of Princess Margaret, Annie B.? I have that magazine here somewhere."

As for Rew, he didn't talk about Andrew Snow for a long time. But one day in January, Rew and I went to Beth's house together, to watch Walter Cronkite on her TV, showing the hostages come home after 444 days in captivity. They were skinny men, with big glasses, dressed in regular clothes and looking hungry. On our way home, I decided to ask Rew if he'd walk with me the next Sunday to see Andrew Snow. And he surprised me and said yes.

We walked through the Zebra Forest. In January, without the leaves, it's wide open there, the snow sky pouring light down on everything, even the brown, sleeping plants. I told Rew about moss that dies away and comes back in summer. I even showed him some, or at least I think that's what it was, soft brown smudges on the base of trees. He didn't say much, but he listened.

To get to Enderfield, you have to come out of the Zebra onto the road, then circle most of the wall and go in through a high mesh gate. At the edge of the Zebra, Rew just stood for a while, arm round an oak tree, picking at the bark.

That bark doesn't peel. I reminded him of that. He stopped.

"You don't have to come if you don't want to," I said. "You can wait here."

So he did, standing in that spot under the bare trees until I came back, so we could walk home together. On the way, I told him how Indian scouts could read direction from the sun.

The next week, he was the one who did the talking. He told me a joke, and it was actually a good one.

"Two muffins were baking in an oven," he said. "And one said to the other, 'Boy, it's hot in here!' And you know what the other one said?"

"Nope."

"It said, 'Eek! A talking muffin!' "

I don't know which one of us was more startled when I laughed.

Above us, the bare branches crisscrossed the sky, the white ones nearly disappearing against the clouds. I thought how much I liked winter in the Zebra, when you can see the intricate pattern of all those twigs and branches, and fat old crows sit at the very tops of the trees like dark winter buds. But then, I like all the seasons, and I like that they'll come round next year, too. It's nice to know, though, that some things really do change. Sometimes jokes can get funnier.

"Back there," Rew said, "does anyone ever say anything funny? Anyone tell jokes?"

"I don't know," I said to him. "I never tried."

He squinted up into a nearby tree, where a couple of withered leaves still hung on, fluttering like flags. "Well, you can tell him the one about the muffins if you want," he said. "That's my new favorite."

And so the next week, I did. Andrew Snow laughed even harder than I had. I didn't know you could laugh in prison.

But actually, you can.

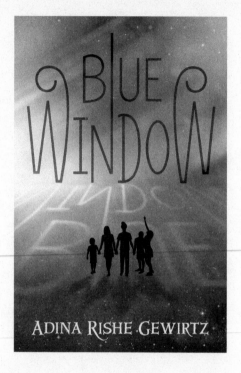